FATAL TEMPTATIONS

FATAL TEMPTATIONS

SHONJERIKA SMILEY

Contents

Chapter One

Chapter One

Ava

Welcome to Jameston.

Three words I didn't realize meant so much to me. It has been six years. Six years since I have driven the narrow roads of my hometown. Six years since I have seen the bright lights of the stadium on a Friday night. Six years since I have seen my family. I hate that it's been so long. In the beginning it was just poor timing. Then my life went to shit, and I couldn't let my family see me that way. I've finally got my life back on track and that's what brings me here. Returning home. This time for good.

I drive straight through town reminiscing on all the memories I have about this place. I keep driving until I reach the street that contains the most memories. The homes riddled with totted wood, broken or boarded up windows are either fixed or torn down. The finally removed the eye sores. The closer I get to my childhood home the more trees I encounter. I see the mailbox with my families address and tun down my once gravel driveway to one that is paved with freshly laid concrete. I almost turn around until I reach a gate with an image my father created when I was a child etched into the gates. What did my parents do now? Ever since my parents signed this new client eight months ago, they have been sounding crazy. A new house is definitely crazy. Talking about accountants and early retirement. How can they afford all of this? I need answers.

I approach the intercom and press the call button. "Who the fuck is you? We ain't ordered shit and didn't invite no fucking body." Yells my Aunt Kat. Momma and Daddy must not be home.

That is the only reason she would be answering the door or in this case the gate.

I distort my voice as much as I can and reply "I have a special delivery for Mr. and Mrs. Moore."

"What is it?"

"I'm not sure ma'am, it says from an Ava Moore." Before I can even complete my name, the gates swing open.

I begin to enter the gate and as I pull up, I hear "Hurry up sha I ain't got all day I'm watching my show." Aunt Kat loves TV. She will watch anything and call it her show even if she just put it on. I steer the box truck with my necessities down the driveway and park in front of the door. As I jump out of the truck the front door opens. "We didn't order a damn" she stops mid-sentence when she realizes who is standing in front of her "...Ava Monique Moore. Now you bring your hoeing ass home."

I try my best to mask the knot that has formed in the pit of my stomach. "You know what, can we go in the house please. These mosquitos eating my ass up."

"What did you say little girl? Don't make me bust you in your mouth. You forgot who you were talking to." I was so used to just talking and I didn't realize what I said. My parents didn't play all that cursing in front of my elders.

"I'm sorry Nanny. I was not trying to be disrespectful."

"I bet. You might be grown but you ain't that grown. Bring yourself in this house before I miss my shows." I follow her into the house. We sit in the love sit and she grabs her coffee before turning to me. "So little girl what brings you home?"

"Well Nanny, I got a promotion. I am now a supervisor." She looks at me with a grin and sips at her cup of coffee. "There was a position open in New Orleans, I wanted to be closer home, so I took it. I am on a vacation until my transfer is complete so I will be around here for a bit."

"Ok. Supervisory Special Agent Ava Moore sounds really nice." I nearly choke on my tongue. That's my title but she shouldn't know that.

"No Nanny I'm not..."

"Hush up child. I already know. You can stop that lying to me."

"Nanny. I don't know what you are talking about."

"Child consultants are not armed in tactical

gear, nor do they arrest people. I still have friends up there from my days in DC. One who just happens to be a receptionist at the bureau. She also told me about Taylor. My heart stops at the name. one I planned to never speak or hear for the rest of my life. "You don't have to say anything right now just know that I'm here when you're ready."

"Oh God, Nanny please don't tell my mom and dad." Just as I thought she had someone following me all these years. Aunt Kat is someone who has connections everywhere.

"Oh, hush child I won't tell your momma, but you need to. Lord knows your momma would have a heart attack and die if something happened to you out there." She was right. If I die my mother would kill herself just to bring me back and kill me herself. That woman has no chill, and everyone knows it. "Speaking of your dramatic ass momma your parents just opened the gate. So, what's the plan? We can't hide that big ass hunk of metal sitting in the driveway."

"I will hide in the pantry. It's time for mom to start making dinner." I followed my aunt so she could show me where the pantry is. It's funny that its technically home but this is the first time I've ever stepped foot in this house. I knew they were planning to remodel, but this is an entirely new house. I am close away just in time. As soon as the door clicks shut my mother's voice can be heard heading our way. "Katherine, where you at?"

"In here." She replies. "Why is there a truck in the driveway and why is your ass in my kitchen."

"The driver got lost so I let them come in to make some calls and Relax Randi, I was just washing my hands."

"Ok now get out.. I'm making Ava's favorite today. She has been on my mind all day" I hear her setting out her bowls and pots then washing her hands. Per her routine she opens the pantry to grab her oil and seasonings. "What the fuck!" in my mother's dramatic fashion she faints. I catch her before she can hit the ground. My mother looks me int the eyes like she seen a ghost. "Hey momma. How are you doing?"

"Alexander! Your daughter in hear trying to kill me."

"Miranda, what you been smoking Ava is…here?" my dad asks shocked to see me holding his prone wife. I help my mom steady to her feet then fall into my dad's large arms. "Micro, what are you doing here girl?"

"I'm back daddy. I'm home." I am wrapped in my parents as they rock me side to side soaking me in tears. "What the hell happened to you all covered drawings and looking like one of them instant hoes." Here she goes. I'm home five minutes and already she is harping on my looks.

"Insta model and I don't know if that is a compliment or not." What does my momma know about Insta? I chat with my parents for a while I try not to mention too much about my job. I mention that I want to surprise my brothers when my momma tells me Junior is oversees on assignment, Tony is a cop ant the other two are in school, in Arix's case college. Since I can't surprise Junior, I start with Tony.

I head to the police station. Tony really became a police officer. I ask for the chief. He quickly approaches me with an off-putting demeanor. "What can I help you with ma'am?"

"This is going to sound really weird, but I need to be let into the back of Antonio Moore's cruiser."

"No ma'am like I told all of the others if he is avoiding you, I am sure it is for good reason." The others? What the hell does my brother have going on around here?

"No, I don't think you understand. My name is Ava Moore. Antonio is my brother. This will be my first time seeing him in six years. I kind of want to surprise him."

"Oh, Well Welcome home. Finally get to meet the infamous Micro. If you will follow me." Why am I infamous? I follow him out to the parking lot, and we approach number 22. "When he first joined the force, everything had to be the number 22 for his lucky charm" He looks at my arm with the number 22 surrounded by flowers tatted on my arm. "I assume that would, be you?" he asks. I was born November 22 at 10:22pm or 22:22 army time. Since young Tony was convinced twenty-two is his lucky number. "Yes Sir." He opens the door and ushers me in the back.

"He should be out any minute now for patrol. I've heard some stories. I will be keeping my eye on you." He shuts the door leaving me alone. I call my parents and let them know what's going on. Just as I finish the call Tony approaches the car. "Finally, some alone time." Once he is settled, he lets out the loudest fart I have ever heard. Then sighs in content. "Motherfucker that's just nasty." I have never seen a Black man so pale unless he was dead. He looks into the rearview mirror. "So, you just crop-dusting criminals that's what you on. That's cruel and unusual punishment. Man, roll down the damn window."

He then jerks around to face me. "What the fuck! Micro, what are you doing here?"

"Came to check on my big bro."

He jumps out of the car, opens my door and pulls me out lifting me into the air. "I missed you girl. Don't you stay gone that long ever again. I don't care what the government needs. We need you more. We at least see Junior every two years and his ass is a marine. Does Ree know you're home?"

"Nope I was going to him next going in birth order. Speaking of when is Junior due back?"

"When I talked to him a couple days ago, he said he wasn't sure but hopefully soon. Come on I'll bring you to meet Ree just let me clock out." He walked back into the building and did whatever he had to and came out in street clothes.

"That was fast."

"I always wear a t-shirt and basketball shorts

under my uniform." I don't have a uniform I think to myself and laugh. "What's so funny?"

"Nothing just things never change." As long as I can remember my brothers changed out of any type of uniform at the first chance they got. We hop into his truck and head to Lafayette to visit Arix, my brother right below me.

Once we arrived, I followed Tony behind very actively trying not to get squashed by all the giants this place seems to have. We enter the dorms and let the desk attendant know what's going on. She calls down who I assume is his RA and we are led to his room. The RA knocks and lets his presence be known before opening the door. We can hear the shower running. "Guest hours end at midnight." He announces before leaving. I make myself comfortable in his lofted bed and scroll through TikTok.

After what seems like forever Arix appears from the bathroom in just a towel. "Hey! Man, what you doing in my room? Oh, is it my turn? Hey beautiful My name is ...aw hell no. Micro what you are doing here?"

"I was visiting my little brother but instead I meet this grown man. What you mean is your turn.

What y'all nasty asses got going on. Y'all sharing pussy now." I hug him tight and say "I wish yall would stop calling me that. I'm not that short."

"To us you are." Says Tony. "This explains why you been acting funny on the phone lately." I feel my phone buzz. I look and see a message from mom saying that Aiden is almost finished with practice.

"Shit, I hate to cut this short, but Aiden is almost finished with practice and I really wanna scare his little ass." My brothers bust out laughing.

"Little my ass. You really been gone too long." Arix says with a mischievous gleam in his eyes. What is that supposed to mean? "Come on I'll take you in my new ride." Arix dresses fully and we quickly make our way to the parking garage where I am met with a massive black truck. "Where in the hell did you get this?"

"Mom and Dad bought it for me a couple weeks ago. You are the first person to ride in it. They don't like how I drive."

"As long as you don't kill me, we are good. I hop in and we take off. I regret my decision. This boy drives like a maniac. If I were on duty, he would be behind bars for reckless driving and a possible DUI. He pulls up to the house and I jump out before he can shut off the car. "Boy I will not be riding with you anymore." I see I am too late Aiden is already here. He is the only one to leave their shoes on the porch. I let Arix walk in front of me so I could hide behind him. I sneak into the hallway and wait in the doorway behind Aiden waiting for the perfect time to announce my presence.

"Man, I'm hungry. Ma when are we eating?"

"Whenever you go wash your hands like I told you too." He quickly runs to the kitchen and washes his hands. I patiently wait for him to sit at the table. "Ma why do you have an extra plate?"

"Because we are having a guest for dinner."

"Aw bruh I don't feel like dealing with people anymore today I'm tired." I walk up behind him and say "That's fine. I'll just head back to DC then."

"Ava!" He stands up and I almost have a heart attack. My baby brother is a giant. He is almost two feet taller than me.

"Aiden what the hell happened to you?" everyone just laughs. I am shocked that my baby brother who I used to carry around the house is almost twice my size.

"If you would have visited in the last six years you would know that I hit a growth spurt at thirteen. Right now, I am six foot six, but the doctors say I'm not done growing yet." I look at him in shock.

"Well, my baby brother is clearly not a baby anymore."

We all sit, eat, and talk until we hear the front door open followed by footsteps. I Look around the table and everyone has a questioning look. I enter my protector mode ready to take out whoever steps through the doorway, I reach to my back for my gun realizing I left it in my car. Fuck. I look around the room from a makeshift weapon then freeze when I see who rounds the corner. My oldest brother who I haven't seen in ten years. Everyone leaps from their chairs embracing him. Tears are falling and excited voices fill the room. I want to run across the room and jump into his arms, but I have to wait my turn. I let everyone get their hugs before I take my turn. I make my way closer to everyone and make eye contact with my dad who steps back and allows me to join the group. I place my hands on my hips and speak, "Hey Junior." My brother looks up and around trying to find the voice. He glances down and stares at me with confusion. "So, you gone leave your sister hanging like that." He lets go of our mom before speaking.

"Micro?" I shake my head. He quickly approaches me and picks me up. I wrap my arms tightly around his neck not ready to let him go. "I missed you so much baby girl." I can't even speak before the tears are falling from my eyes. This day couldn't have gone any better. A feeling of peace washes over me. I'm home.

2

Chapter Two

Chapter Two

Dare

"Little girl, are you crazy put the gun down."

"No tell me who you are."

"You are the one trespassing why don't you tell me who you are?"

"I'm tired of this back-and-forth shit either you tell me what you want or I'm putting another whole in you. Take your pick talk or die."

"I'm not telling you shit." The next thing I know is a bright light illuminates the room.

T wo months earlier

I hear a knock at my door. I motion for them to come in. "Mr. Jones." Says my assistant James. "Everyone is waiting for you in the conference room."

"I'll be right there James." I gather my things and head to the conference room. I enter the room and all talking ceases. "Good afternoon, everyone. I know it's Friday and everyone wants to go home so I will try to keep this short. We have been low in sales this quarter, so I want to shake things up a little. Nothing major, but noticeable. Production I need you all to bring me at least one new product idea. Marketing I need new ads on my desk or in my inbox. Finance, please try to save my money. Public relations put out some feelers to ring in more sales. You all have until close of day next Friday to have something on my desk or in my inbox. That's two weeks people. If for some reason that can't be done let me know and I'll find you another place to work, because it won't be here." I look at the faces in the room and see a few who I can already tell are going to be a problem. "Any questions? It doesn't have to be about this specifically."

One of my more seasoned employees raises her

hand. "Mr. Jones is it true that you plan on expanding the company?"

"Yes, Charlotte. I plan to open my own stores instead of having to go through others. We will have a Daring Delights storefront opening soon. I plan to make a trip soon to choose where I want to open the first five stores. Anything else?"

I see a member of the test group raise her hand. "Can we submit ideas even if we aren't apart of the previously mentioned departments."

Before I can answer the troublesome Marcus mutters assuming I can't hear. "No. You sluts are only good enough to use the toy, not make them. That's why we have designers." The woman lowers her head and rapidly blinks to hide the tears.

I stand from my chair and approach Marcus. I grab him by the shirt and raise him to meet my eyes. "Don't you ever speak to a woman like that again in your life especially not in my presence. I wouldn't have to ask for more ideas if the job was being done. For that, you're fired. Pack your things and get out of my building, and don't you think about using me for a reference." I drop him back into the chair. "You have 30 minutes to vacate the premises before I call the police. Does anyone else feel the same way? If so, you can go. I have zero tolerance for disrespect in my business. They are more important to this company than the rest of you in here. Which is why they are paid more."

I see the men turn red with anger. "What do you mean they are more important than us. There would be no toys for them to use if it weren't for us?"

"You may create the devices; however, these people risk their lives placing high speed electronic moving parts in or near the most sensitive parts of their bodies. Pair with the constant humiliation they may feel from all of you, they deserve the higher pay. If you had the balls to strip naked and play with sexually stimulating toys while being recorded and watched by six other people, be my guess." I turned my attention to the rest of the room. "Now if we have no other productive questions meeting adjourned." I begin to exit the room before I remember I just opened a new position. "Before I forget let your friends know we are now hiring."

I walk into my office and sit in my seat. I then hear a small knock at my door. "Come in."

"Mr. Jones." I hear Aaliyah the tester who asked about submissions say. "How can I help you?"

"Thank you for what you did. Me and the others appreciate it."

"No problem. If any other comments like that are made, let me know. I'll take care of it. Is there anything else I could help you with?"

"Yes sir. There is. I was wondering if I could be more involved with the production of the toys. I know you already have a team of great designers, and this is not what you hired me for but there are some changes to the older and any newer model toys that could bring greater pleasure and saving you money. You could reduce production costs and receive a greater profit while helping the planet. Boosting your approval with the public."

"Really. Why don't you gather up your findings and present them to me?" She reaches into her briefcase and hands me a file. "I already have." Wow she was prepared. I flip through the presentation she has prepared. "I have a secondary model for every toy you have ever produced. We could re-introduce the older toys with these modifications as a special edition for a limited time raising the original price. We could also do partnership with some erotic authors. So that we could sell bundle deals in the new stores bringing in a new customer base. I was also thinking of a plastic rally. You bring in a bag of plastic and get ten percent off your purchase" With these ideas I could use old, recycled material melt it down and configuring a new structure making more durable and long-lasting toys for less. Keeping more of it out the landfills and oceans. She even has a battery exchange option where customers can turn in their dead batteries for a discount on new ones. "How old are you Aaliyah?"

"I just turned eighteen, sir." I am shocked when I hear her say that. I knew she was young but not that young.

"You are eighteen and have only been with us for two months and you just became a great asset. How would you like a new position as Vice President of Merchandise and Sales? I was going to announce the opening of the new position at a later date, but you are exactly what I am looking for."

"Oh no sir there must be someone else more qualified than me. I have a month left in school. High school."

"Which makes you that much more remarkable. Do you plan on attending college?"

"No Sir. Although you pay me very generously after taking care of my mom and siblings, I don't have enough money for tuition."

"Well, how about you apply to any college you desire. I will take care of your expenses on top of your regular salary. You can work for me on a remote basis, and I can fly you in if needed."

"Are you serious?"

"Very much. You are going to be the secret weapon that takes this company to the top. How about you think about it and let me know? If you turn down V, I will still send you to college, I will write you an excellent recommendation letter to any place you like. I think you could do remarkable things in this world and a degree will help get your foot into the door to make that happen."

"Thank you, Mr. Jones."

"No, Thank you Aaliyah. You just put more money in everyone's pockets with this proposal including yours. Now get out of here and enjoy your Friday night. I'll see you Monday morning."

"You too sir." She replies as she packs up her things and hurried out of my office. I get my lawyer on my phone to get her contract ready. I hang up with my lawyer and my phone begins ringing. I see that it is my best friend Arix Moore. "Hey man. What's up?"

"Nothing much how about you. I was going to call you later. How do you feel about making a little more money from your books?"

"I'm doing really good right now. I don't think you can make my sales get any higher."

"I beg to differ my friend. How would you like to sell a few copies of each book of your series paired with a Daring Device in my new Daring Delights stores?"

"You're branching out on your own? That's great man. No more money-hungry distributors with their hands in your pockets. I never thought of that. Let me talk with my agent and publisher and get back to you on that. I actually called to ask you a favor."

"Sure, what is it?"

"Well, my parents planned a family vacation for the close of summer and they need someone to house sit for them. All of our people have plans and can't take a month out of their plans to house sit."

"You want me to fly all the way to Louisiana to housesit."

"Yeah man that's what best friends do."

"Did you forget your best friend is the CEO and founder of an up-and-coming Adult entertainment business. I just closed a deal with the number one porn distribution service to agree to use my toys in their professional films. I have to make sure I have everything they want."

"That is exactly why you need the break. We leave June 28th. You could use it as your own vacation away from work."

"You waited to the last minute and couldn't find anyone else, could you?" 12 "No. Everyone has already made plans and I told Me that I would handle it. "Fine. I should have everything in order by then."

"Thank you. You are a life saver. My mom would kill me if I didn't find someone to watch the place especially after the remodel. These kids would love to try to have a party in the place."

"Wait is your sister going with y'all?"

"No. A, Is still in D.C. It would take an act of congress to get that woman back here. How is a consultant so busy she can't come home occasionally? I mean I understand in college she needed to work during breaks, but she didn't even tell us she graduated. Who doesn't invite their family that has always loved and supported them to their graduation? Then even after graduation she never came home. It's been two years! She should have some vacation time to visit us. I mean what is going on? Does she have a kid or something? She was killed and there is someone pretending to be her, so we don't know she is gone?" I choose then to interrupt him. "OK Ree, I now realize where you get the material for your book. You have a wild imagination. She is a woman in a predominantly male world. She probably doesn't want to seem weak. Take it from me the business world can be cutthroat. Speaking of the women in your life. How is your online girlfriend is doing?"

"She is not my girlfriend. We are pen pals. She lives across the country. How about you and that girl Aaliyah?"

"Nope. I don't like what you are insinuating. I think of her as my little sister she reminds me of myself. She just left my office. She is still in high school but has better business ideas and better head on her shoulders than most of my graduate degree. If she plays her cards right, she'll be on the fast track to president. I need someone like her to take my company to new levels and run the company when I need a vacation."

"You have a minor testing out sex toys? Man do you want to go to jail."

"Relax dog she is eighteen. I checked her file. I am covered legally, and I received a waiver from her mother. I can't believe you would think so badly of me."

"Your close enough was probably days out from her 18th birthday when you hired her." I glance at her file and he's right. She applied on her 18th birthday and was hired two days later. "How long? I know you just checked so, how long after her birthday was, she hired?"

"It doesn't matter she…"

"How long Dare?"

"Two days."

"Two Days! The girl didn't even have time for adulthood to sink in yet. "Hey, she got an eighty-one-thousand-dollar salary as a late birthday gift."

"You pay your girls thirty-one thousand dollars to have orgasms all day?"

"Technically she gets about forty thousand

because she is part - time. And They don't orgasm all day. They put themselves at risk of using faulty equipment. One day we had to send a girl to the ER because one of our licking toys malfunctioned. The silicone tore and one of the support mechanisms was exposed and cut her two centimeters from her clit. Thank God for waivers. Her husband, however, was not happy. She needed stitches. After that she quit. She has a new baby last time I heard. I sent a bouquet of flowers and a thousand dollars as baby gift."

"See if people didn't know you like I do they would think you were completely crazy and perverted."

"Yeah. Well, I'm going to head home. You need me for the twenty-eighth, right?"

"Thanks man. If my agent agrees we can sign a contract to package a shipment of books for a pleasure pal, then we will be even."

"We are not calling them that. Go write something talk to you soon."

"Alright man bye." I look down at my desk and can't wait for this vacation.

3

Chapter Three

Chapter Three

Ava

I love how my mother forgets about a month-long vacation. I can't really blame her because I did show up the day before they were to leave. She didn't remember until the car came to pick them up. her procrastination got the best of her as usual and she was the only one not packed. they were all in a frenzy this morning. It wasn't until I went down to eat breakfast that everyone remembered I was there. The oh shit look on my dad's face was priceless. It got even better when Junior walked down after me.

He had to return to base, and I volunteered to watch the place while they were gone. I honestly didn't want to go anywhere. I decided to clean up today. I saved Aiden's room for last because I don't know his cleaning habits. When I left mom was still doing the hard work for him. I open the door and wonder when the last time he seen the floor. I threw everything to the floor in a pile and worked from there. I was in for a huge shock when I got to his medicine cabinet. An empty box of condoms. A generic brand at that. My baby brother just lost his virginity. I cried. I added magnums to my shopping list.

After cleaning the mirror, I looked at myself and I don't like what I see in the mirror. Yes, my body was in peak condition, but you wouldn't be able to tell by looking at me. My once luscious thick hair looked like a damn Brillo pad. My warm honey skin was now ashen and flaky. I walked back into my bedroom to look in my full-length mirror. I shed my clothes to really see myself. My body hair had grown wild. that explains the stronger body odor. I try to think back to the last time I took the time to pamper myself. That would be right before I graduated college three years ago. I've been so busy trying to save everyone else I've neglected myself. That's it. I put on a simple outfit. Hop into my car and head into town.

First, to a nail salon and get a nice acrylic mani-pedi. I get everything polished white. I enjoy my leg massage which makes me add a full body massage to my list. I go online and find one in Lafayette and make the appointment for later today.

I then head to Walmart. I head straight to the HBA section. I grab some good shampoo and conditioner along with a hair mask and deep conditioner. I grab a moisturizing body wash along with some in shower lotion. I refuse to continue to neglect myself. I even splurge on a big bottle of bubble bath. I also pass and grab Aiden's little gift. I walk over to the home section and grab a few candles. I head to checkout and still feel like I'm missing something, a silk robe. I head to the lingerie store and grab a black lace bra and panty set. I grab a few other things and head to my spa appointment.

I walk into the place and am instantly calmed. I follow the sign and take off my shoes. Soft carpeting at my feet. Enveloping my feet in a hug. The windows are all covered in blackout curtains. The room is lit by small lamps and candles. The smell of fresh cotton in the air. The sound of soft waves in the background. "Hello, I'm Ava Moore. I have an appointment."

"Yes, follow me." I'm escorted down the hall, and we stop in front of a room where she ushers me inside before closing the door behind me. This room smells of teakwood or a fine ass Black man as I like to say. There is a large massage table in the center of the room and a curvy brownskin in the corner.

"Hi. I'm sorry. Where you ready for me?"

"Yeah, I was... Ava?"

"Omg Payge. Hey how are you?"

"I'm good. I didn't know you were back in town."

"I didn't know you were back either. Figures your crazy ass would be the hulk."

"Hulk?"

"It's what we call the clients who schedule the service you did. Full body wax, acupuncture, and a deep tissue massage. Only someone who is incredibly angry with a high pain tolerance can take more that all in one day."

"Not angry, a mild pain tolerance. I wax myself all the time I just decided to go to a professional to pamper myself."

"Good well let's get started." The anxiety I felt when I scheduled the appointment leaves as I have someone I know and trust touching me. For the next hour, my high school best friend who I haven't seen in almost eight years was up close and personal with my body. We start with her ripping every hair out of my body except my head. I have a second of when I thought she took my pussy off with that wax. "Motherfucker." She just laughs as she cleans up and plucks the hairs that were too stubborn to come out with the others.

She then tuns down the lights and has me lay down for my massage. She rubs me down and pays close attention to all of my really sore spots. I fell asleep part of the way through. I woke to her turning on the lights and informing me that she will begin my acupuncture services. I sit as still as I can while she places needles up my back and legs. She became hesitant when she reached the scars along my hip partially covered in tattoos. I knew she had questions, but I shook my head not wanting to talk about it. We fall into conversation as if it hasn't been nearly a decade since she left town. Once she removes the needles I feel like a new woman. Not one who runs around the country searching for missing kids, but one who spends her days shopping and planning parties. Her voice snaps me out of my day dram. "We should get together outside of me torturing you. Maybe we can talk about what happened in DC that left you all scarred up. My number hasn't changed. Call me." I leave floating and feeling much better. I think I'll take the long way home.

On the way home I see a lot for sale. Six acres surrounded by trees 80,000 dollars. Across town from my parents which isn't saying much. I enter the number in my phone and continue home. I'll call them later. I gather everything out of the car and head into the house. I look at my phone. 6 o'clock. Damn I've been gone seven hours. I need some dinner. I head in the kitchen and put together a quick shrimp fettuccine. I also put some catfish filets to marinate. Then I preheat the oven for some garlic bread. I let everything sit with my heat on low. And head to the bathroom to prepare my bath.

I place candles around the room and place a

lighter next to a candle. I then fold a towel on the counter. I grab the bags from my trip out and bring them into the bathroom. I place my shampoo and all my other bath goodies onto the built-in shelves. I grab a pair of soft slippers and place them next to the bathmat. I re-enter my bedroom and set out my panty set on the bed next to my robe and a pair of Louis Vuitton stilettos for a little photographic fun. I quickly finish cooking and eat my wonderful meal. Damn I can cook. To finish everything off I fix myself a glass of wine and take the bottle into the bathroom with me. I turn on the water to have a nice hot bath. I add my soothing lavender scented bubble bath and turn on the jets. I undress and slowly lower myself into the water. "Hey Siri play My Jams Playlist."

"Now Playing My Jams Playlist on Apple Music" I relax as I hear J. Cole pump through my speakers. I submerge my head into the water. I let my hair soak and loosen before lifting myself up. I pump a generous amount of shampoo into my hands working up the product into a lather I can feel the stress of these past few years lift away. I make a silent vow to not let myself get like this ever again.

The next thing I know is the water is cold and my playlist is finished. Damn I must have been tired I guess that massage nap wasn't enough. I quickly finish my bath and head into my bedroom. I moisturize my body and put on my outfit.

As I'm taking pictures, I hear the door chime meaning someone has entered the house. Now who the fuck just let themselves in my house. I quickly throw on my robe and grab my gun. They gone be sorry they chose this house to break into. I quietly make my way down the stairs. I search until I find someone standing in our home theater. "I will give you five seconds to get the hell out of here before I shoot." At the sound of my voice, he turns around. Once he sees the gun pointed at him, he freezes. "Hey! You're not supposed to be here shorty." He yells. Almost like he is disciplining me. "No, you're not supposed to be here now, get the hell out of here."

"I don't know who you are sweetheart, but I don't think your parents would be happy to know that their little girl is in someone's house with a gun. Now put the gun down and we can get you back home and give your daddy his gun back." *What is this man talking about?* "You know what you must not understand the words that are coming out of my mouth so let me show you some action." I walk closer to him, cock the gun, and aim. "Little girl, are you crazy put the gun down."

"Call me a little girl one more time. I double dog dare you. Now tell me the who you fucking are?"

"You are the one trespassing why don't you tell me who you are?" *What is this dude talking about? How am I trespassing?* "I'm tired of this back and forth. either you tell me what you want or I'm putting another whole in your head. Take your pick."

"I'm not telling you shit." Before he can fully finish his sentence, I pull the trigger. The bullet goes flying and I hit my target dead on. He lays on the floor completely motionless until he realizes he wasn't hit. He jumps to his feet in relief and then anger. "That's it I'm calling the cops your little ass is going to jail."

"Call them. I'll call and tell them you are threatening an FBI agent thy will love that."

"Li- What are you talking about?" As if by magic the landline rings. I keep my weapon trained on him as I place the call on speaker. "Hello Moore residence. Ava speaking."

"Ava Monique the neighbors just called telling me they heard gunshots coming from our house. Are you okay?"

"I'm fine Ma. We have a little situation, but I have it under control."

"Wait you're Ava?" I look at him confused. How does he know me? "Yes. Now who are you?"

"Darrius Jones. I'm friends with Arix. Ask your mothers she knows who I am." "Momma do you know a Darrius Jones?"

"Yeah. That's Ree's little friend why." I lowered my gun in relief. "Because he is standing in front of me about to be shot." As I am talking to my mother his phone rings. "Arix. Man, I will kick your ass."

"Ava, did you say shot. What is going on over there?"

"Long story short I thought he broke in, so I shot at him. On that note I owe you a new window."

"Arix Monroe boy. I thought you called Dare and told him not to come. I'm sorry baby girl you must have been so scared." Once she knows I'm okay she switches to anger. "You better have that gun out of my house before I get home Ava."

"Yes ma'am. I'll talk to you later the police just pulled up." I take out the clip and place it in my other hand. I go to let the police in. "Hello Miss Moore. We have a report of shots fired. Is everything ok?"

"Yes officer. Just a misunderstanding." I explain to him what happened. He looks at me skeptically. "Can we see the other party to ensure that he is unharmed?"

"Mr. Jones the police would like to speak to you." I call out. He quickly enters the foyer and addresses the cops. "I'm fine officers a little shook up but no bodily harm."

"Are you ok staying here with Miss Moore or do you need to be escorted to a safer location."

"He'll be fine. I was protecting my home. I wasn't even aiming at him it was a warning shot." they look to Darrius for reassurance. He nods and I quickly usher them out the door before they can respond. "Goodnight officers."

"How would you like something drink?"

"Sure. You owe me on after almost shooting me." He follows behind me to the kitchen. I place my gun on the counter, I enter the pantry and unlock my parents liquor fridge. I make us both cocktails and join him at the island. I raise my glass and say "Truce." He nods his head and takes a sip. "Why did you keep calling me little girl."

"At first glance you look like a little girl. After that, I focused on the gun you had pointed at me. It wasn't until you said your name that I looked at you and seen you are far from a child." His eyes sweep over my body reminding me I am sitting in my parents kitchen half naked. He raised his glass and murmured "I can give you a child though."

"Excuse me?"

"Nothing."

"Mmmm hmm" I continue sipping my drink looking at the fine dark specimen before me. If he weren't so cocky I would let him hit. I finish my drink before placing my glass in the sink. I then make my way upstairs. "Goodnight Mr., Jones."

Dare

Goodnight Mrs. Jones.

4

Chapter Four

Chapter Four

Unknown

The time has come. I've waited long enough. I search through the roster and see who would fit his criteria the best. I the see there is an agent just transferring to the New Orleans field office. She's perfect. Sorry Ava your vacation is over.

Darrius

Living with Ava these last few weeks has been absolute hell. The woman was walking sin. It wasn't until I seen her the next morning that I realized how short she is. The woman is tiny. She is made to be protected yet she is the protector. We have fallen into a routine. I get up and put on a pot of coffee before taking my shower. Then she wakes up and makes breakfast. We go through the day like two old friends or a married couple. I have learned so much about her this last month. She hates a mess. things have to be done her way or are they wrong? She is allergic to footwear. I have only seen her wear shoes when she is leaving the house. Her feet are probably rough as hell. I made a last-minute trip to California and when I return, I see a taxi in the driveway. Arix, and his folks are back. As I get closer, I see two other cars that I don't recognize. I find a place to park and head inside. I am greeted with everyone sitting in the living room. "Hey everybody." I wave and place my keys on the hook. "Who's rides outside. No disrespect but them bitches nice."

"Oh, that's Ava's. They came in earlier. I don't know why that child needs two cars, especially an SUV. She is too small to be driving that massive thing."

"I think it fits her." She needs a big car to hold her attitude. I go to join them on the couch. And see Ava in the kitchen "I mean she drives something she is used to being an..."

"Darrius" calls Ava interrupting me. "Come see I need your help." I'm confused so I go meet her. "One second everyone. Woman, what is wrong with you?"

"Are you trying to get me killed?'

"What are you talking about?"

"They don't know what I do for a living. They think I'm a consultant remember. If they knew the truth, they would worry about me and make me stress too much to do my job. So don't say anything." Before I can say anything, Antonio joins us. "What yall got going on here?" he looks between me and Ava waiting on an answer. "Nothing much. Ava wanted me to taste her food. He looks back and forth between us before saying "mhmm. That's all it better be."

"What's that supposed to mean?" She asks. "It means. Arix told me all about this dude. I don't want you hanging around him."

"The last time I checked I was grown. So, I decide who I associate myself with." She walks off and joins the rest of her family in the living room. "Look man just do us all a favor and leave her alone. She doesn't need the problems you bring. Understand?" I look him in the eye and calmly say. "Like she said she's grown." I then return to the living room to listen to the Moores' tales of their vacation. "... So, I was relaxing in my room just chilling talking on the phone with this shorty I met at the beach a couple of days before when this retard comes into my room talking like a female and pissing her off." Says Arix pointing at Aiden. "Payback is a mother ain't it."

"What are you talking about?"

"Last year. I was on the phone with Ashley, and you just had to yell that Chrys was here to see me."

"You had company. I was letting you know."

"She was standing in my room. I knew she was there. You just wanted to start problems. You knew she didn't like me hanging with Chrys. She was convinced we were more than friends."

"Ok but didn't you and Chrys start dating like two weeks later."

"What does that have to do with anything?"

"Had I not messed things up with her you and Chrys would still be just friends right now. Maybe not even that. You're welcome." Aiden launches a pillow at him. "Ok. So, who is this Chrys y'all talking about?" asks Ava. "Aid's little girlfriend. They are inseparable. Matter of fact that's probably her coming up the driveway now." Says Mr. Moore. The conversation continues as the front door opens and the pretty little light skin in question walks in. Instead of hi, she yells "really Aiden this is how you treat me?" Everyone looks at her confused and then I see the problem. Ava looks like a teenager, and Aiden has his arms wrapped around her waist prevent her from tickling him, but to anyone else it would look like a couple snuggled together on the couch. Aid quickly explains. "Chrys it is really not what you think. This is Ava." Once he says that her face registers a resemblance. Ava and Aiden look the most alike. "

Oh my God I'm so embarrassed. Amanda showed me some girl in your snap story. I didn't even stop to actually look at who she was I just came straight here. I'm so sorry y'all." Aiden pushes Ava off him, and she lands on the floor hard then approaches Chrystina. He pulls her to Ava and says "Babe. This is my annoying little big sister. Ava Monique Moore. Micro this is Chrystina. Despite the unfortunate outburst she reminds me of you." Ava gives a tight hello before approaching Chrys.

"If you ever come into my momma's house like that again. I will beat your little ass. Comprende?"

She doesn't speak she just shakes her head and sits on the floor between Aiden's legs. "Hello, everyone. Welcome back." The Moore's mumble their greetings. Ava plops herself next to me and her next move shocks me she lays her head on my lap and starts playing on her phone like its nothing. We all sit in silence for what seems like forever. Her Mother looks at us and grins and whispers in her husband's ear. He looks at us before speaking. "So, Dare what did you and Ava get into while we were gone?"

"Besides her almost shooting me nothing. I looked around at possible locations for my new store. I have this author who is willing to collab with me for these bundle deals to help boost sales. I'm actually thinking of moving my company headquarters. L.A. has given me all that it can. I'm not quite sure where yet. I'll be talking to my lawyers to start the process sometime this week."

"That's great son."

"Now Ava. Would you like to explain to everyone why you had a gun in this house?"

"Ya sees what had happened was. I've been

living alone for the past three years so I figured I needed some protection. Don't worry I moved them into my truck when it got here."

"Them, how many guns do you have?" "Do y'all hear that? My phone is ringing. I'll talk to all later." She then sprints up the stairs. "Well, I'm going to change and head out back to shoot some hoops if that' ok with everyone else." I practically run up the stairs. I quickly change into something more comfortable. As I leave my room, I nearly run into Arix in the hallway. "How about we play a little one on one."

"Okay lets go." We hop on the elevator ad ride down to the first floor. We grab some towels and bottles of water before making our way to the back yard. Even though I've been here numerous times it still never shocks me how big this place is. We place our things on the little bench they have beside the court.

We begin playing and as always, I'm beating his ass. We play for a while until he can't breathe "Back to what you mentioned earlier. I talked to my publisher, and they think it's a great idea. I have a new series coming up, so we decided to release it all at once each book paired with a toy that will be mentioned in the novel. Like an interactive experience. We are shooting for this time next year. How does that sound?"

"Great man. I'll email Aaliyah ad have her talk to the design team to see what they can come up with. I'll send you samples you can choose from, and we'll go from there."

"Alright sounds like a plan."

"Now that business is out of the way. How are things with you and your mystery girl?"

"Everything's fine. She is taking summer classes right now, so we don't get to talk as much as we usually do. Her dad is still an asshole. I wish she would just move out already. I hate seeing her so miserable."

"I know, but she must have her reasons."

"I guess you're right. He better be lucky I don't know where they live. I'd kick his ass."

"I feel you man but don't be doing noting drastic. We don't need you in headlines just yet ok."

"I hear you. When are you going to find a lady? You haven't dated since I've known you."

"Well, your sister is fine as hell what is her situation?"

"You are funny." He looks at me and realizes I'm not joking. "you are too. Did you fuck my sister?"

"You know me better than that. Plus, I barely know her."

"That hasn't stopped you before. I promise your ass if you try anything with my sister not only will that be the end of our friendship it will be the end of your life." I look him in the eyes and see something that makes me realize the ugly side of Arix is rearing his head again. I remember that fateful day two and a half years ago. It was his second year at UL. I was finishing my masters. I was walking through Legacy Park apartments when I hear yelling further down the parking lot. I try to ignore it until I hear a woman scream. I turn and investigate. Once the scene comes into view, I see two men fighting. More accurately a ma getting his ass beat. I see that he stops fighting and lies prone on the pavement. I jump in and stop him from possibly killing him if he hasn't already. "what's going on over here?"

"This motherfucker thought he could punk me. He was being highly disrespectful making on my woman when I'm standing right here. He thought

I was coward had to show his ass ain't nothing coward about me."

"Well, I think you showed him a little too much. "I squat down to see if the man has a pulse. This man is holding on for dear life." I pull out my phone and call 911. You better get out of here before they show up or you are going to jail. He runs off with his girl. I assume I'll never see him again but imagine my surprise when he is sitting one of my students. He stayed after begging me not to turn him in. I agreed as long as he promised to get help with his anger. He went for months but I don't think it took. I hear the patio door open and see Ava prance out in her string bikini. My dick instantly starts to brick up then I see the doorway darken. Tony is standing in the door eyes daring me to try something. My dick shrinks like I was doused in ice water.

5

Chapter Five

Chapter Five

Ava

I wake to my alarm blaring in my ear. I almost hit the snooze button until I remember what today is. My first assignment as supervisor. My joke the other day was true my phone really was ringing. Apparently, a high-profile child has gone missing, and no ransom demand was made so I got called in. Why me I haven't even taken my position yet. It wouldn't be so bad if my meeting weren't in DC. If I don't get up now, I'll be late for my flight.

I finally get out the bed and prepare for what

I already know will be a long day. I lay out my clothes and run my bath. I grab my phone and quickly choose a playlist to get me up and moving. I grab my suitcase and place it by my door. I also place my purse and all carry-on items on top. I don't want to forget anything. I return to my bathroom and strip out of my clothing. I then slowly lower myself into my hot bath. I quickly go through my routine to make sure my skin is glowing to give myself a little extra confidence in the meeting. I just hope I don't mess up what might be my biggest assignment yet. Once I'm finished, I walk into my bedroom to air dry. I am applying lotion when I hear a knock at my door. Before I can answer the door is pushed open, I cover myself with my hands as best as I can. These 34F breasts don't make that an easy feat. "Hey, Ava the driver ... oh shit I'm sorry." Quickly Dare turns around. "Your mom sent me to make sure you were awake."

"I am 24 years old. That woman has to realize I am plenty capable of getting myself up in the morning."

"Also, the driver called to say he had a family emergency, and he can't take you to the airport. Do you need me to drive you?"

"Why can't anyone else take me?"

"Your parents and Antonio are at work, Arix and Aid at school."

"It's Wednesday. I completely forgot everyone went back today. I'll be ready in a second."

"Yeah, sorry. I'll be in the kitchen." He closes the door and I continue getting ready. I finish getting dressed. I gather my hair into a ponytail. I walk over to my closet and open my newly installed safe which holds my gear. I put on my hip and shoulder holsters, and I'll arm myself when I get outside. I almost close the safe before grabbing my badge. I take a good photo. I am one sexy bitch. I grab my jacket and my suitcase and other trivial things and head downstairs. I enter the kitchen and Dare is on the phone. "Aaliyah, slow down sweetie. Have you made your decision? Good. Now send me a copy of all the forms and I'll meet you at the apartment to finish everything. Alright I will see you tomorrow morning. Bye." He looks up and sees me and nearly jumps out of his skin. "Make some noise woman damn about to give me a heart attack."

"Sorry I didn't want to interrupt your phone call." I couldn't hide the judgmental tone in my voice. I have no right to be jealous. We are just friends. I wouldn't even say that we are room-mates. "I'm ready to go if you are."

"Yeah. Let's go." I put a little extra sway to my hips knowing he is watching me. I quickly grab my guns from my car then place my luggage in the trunk and make myself comfortable. Time to get all this over with. We make ourselves comfortable and get on the road. I must give off an attitude because without me making a sound Daniel says. "Are you jealous?"

"What are you talking about boy?" I ask trying to play stupid. "You're not dumb. You know what I'm talking about."

"Did you just call me dumb." Why do I always have to start an argument? "No, I said you are not dumb no stop trying to start an argument. Every conversation with you so far has been an argument do you not get tired of being mad? Every time I speak her name you get nasty. Since you won't ask. Aaliyah is an eighteen-year-old employee. She is my newest VP in operation. once I get the paper-work from her tomorrow when I go back home."

"A VP at eighteen who did she fuck to get that job?"

"Herself." Ava looks at me with confusion. "She

was one of the testers. She presented a proposal for a new cost-effective line of toys. I offered her the job on the spot. Now you can explain why you have to rush off to DC unexpectedly."

"It's expected of me I've known I was going to be called soon. My vacation ended two weeks ago. I was just waiting for my paperwork to clear. I just want to know why the new DC unit chief isn't taking this case. I'm going to sleep. I had maybe three hours of sleep." My statement is confirmed when I let out the biggest yawn. I quickly doze off. He drops me at the airport, and I fall back asleep as soon as the plane leaves the runway.

After two hours in a car and four hours on a plane. I'm ready to stretch my legs. I grab a taxi to my hotel and get settled before finally heading to the office. I enjoyed my leave but now it's back to the hustle and bustle. I enter the department and head straight to my temporary office. On it in a box are several good well cards and welcome back cards. I even have a dead bouquet of roses. The real reason I was on "vacation" hits me and ruins my good mood. I place my coat on my chair and before I get a chance. I am summoned. "Moore conference room."

"Yes sir." I get up and head down the hall. "As you know this case extremely high profile. I don't know why he chose you, but he must have seen your potential or something."

"Wait I was requested by who sir. I haven't been briefed on the case yet."

"You are looking for a missing teen."

"Ok so why all the secrecy." He motions for me to follow him. We approach one of the interview rooms which is heavily guarded. "These are the girl's parents." I look inside and sitting at the table looking completely sick is non-other the President of the United States and the First lady. "Wait the first daughter is missing? How the hell does someone kidnap the first daughter and not get caught by the secret service."

"That is why you are here. Get in there." I compose myself and prepare for the case of my life. I enter the room and switch to business mode. "Hello, I'm Supervisory Special Agent Ava Moore. I'm going to find your daughter. Can you tell me the last time you saw her?"

"Yes. It was a week from today. She had come home from school, and we called her into our room. She had forgotten to do something before school. I can't even remember what it was now. I told her to go to room and put her electronics on my dresser because I was late for a meeting." Says the first lady. "when I didn't see anything, I went to her room to take them, and he was gone. I looked and asked around, but no one had seen her. It's when we checked the cameras and seen her ushered into a van that we realized she was taken."

"I need to look in her bedroom. If that would be, ok?"

"Yes, we haven't let anyone option for them to lead the way. "We need every second if we are going to find her especially with the assailant having a week head-start she could quite literally be any-where." inside since we realized she was gone."

"Well let's go." I stand and me and my team load up and follow behind the motorcade to the white house. I am escorted to the room and begin our work. I take pictures of the room from every angle before I move anything. I then turn off the lights and use a black light to see for blood. Thankfully, there is none. I look at her desk and see that her laptop is open but off. I tap the mouse pad and see she doesn't have a password. I look through it and see that there is nothing on it except a few school assignments all uploaded and updated the day she went missing. "So, either she completely cleared her hard drive, or this isn't her computer. I would also guess that the best buy receipt and slapped on vinyl this is a decoy. Her real computer is with her. I'm going to tag this for evidence." I gather the laptop and everything on her desk in bags to look at later. I look through her drawers and find a stack of printed emails stashed in a binder dating back a year. "Who is AM337?" And why would she print off e-mails? "That would be her pen pal Erick or something like that. They met on some website for school and became best friends. He is partially the reason I asked you. He is from Louisiana. I just don't know what part. She yelled something about meeting him during the fight before she went missing."

"Well, that was a big lead. I'll have everything shipped to my new office in New Orleans and start the search."

"Actually, we need this to be highly confidential. Any chance you could work this from home. The ease of her being taken we don't know how deep the assailants grasp is."

"Understandable, I will also need a copy of

all security tapes from up to a week before she disappeared. Everything that isn't confidential of course."

"Consider it done. The tapes will be sent to your room. Just let us know anything else you may need. I want my baby back." Says the President. "Yes Mr. President."

"Please call me Malcom."

"And I'm Amanda "

"Alright Malcom and Amanda. I will keep in touch. I need to get to your finding your daughter. Let me know if there is anything."

"Thank You." I gather the boxes of evidence I have accumulated and head back to my office. I delegate smaller tasks to some members of my team while the rest work other cases. My gut tells me this case will be one to remember and not in a good way. How does the first daughter disappear? Who waits a week to report their child missing?

6

❧

Chapter Six

Chapter Six

Darrius

I find myself back in Jameston. This time for good. California has served its purpose and it's time to move on. I decide to spend some time with Arix and his folks before I decide my next move. I have spent the last two weeks getting everything together. I managed to rent a house and set up a temporary office, and get Aaliyah settled into her new position. She is staying in California until we find a new office to be closer to keep an eye on the production of her new line. Once the nerves wear off, I think she will be a force to be reckoned with. I head to the kitchen to fix myself a snack and remember. I haven't gone grocery shopping yet. I call Mrs. Moore to get a mother's opinion on what to get since my own mother died five years ago. "Momma Randi is there chance you would like to make groceries with me? I have no idea what to get besides the basics."

"Oh, Sweetie I wish I could but I'm on my way to a meeting. How about I send one of the kids to your house with my list and they can go with you to help."

"That works. I'm headed to Wal-Mart have them meet me by the dairy section."

"Ok baby. She is on her way."

"She? No not Ava." I'm too late she already hung up. Shit well I can't just tell her don't come I really need that list. Well now I have to get dressed. I hurry and throw on some clothes and head out of the door. I quickly find a spot near the front of the store. I receive a text rom Ava saying that says meet in the dairy section. I entered the store grabbing a basket and walking straight to the dairy section. I see her dressed similar to me holding what I assume is the grocery list. "So where do we start?"

"Well hello to you too Darrius."

"I'm sorry I'm starving. Hello Ava. Where do we start?"

"I will take the front half you take the back we will meet at the registers." She takes the list and takes a picture of it before walking away. I shop in silence and make a good time getting everything on the list and more before I realize I made it to the same aisle as Ava. I start to approach her when I see her talking to a couple. I get closer to listen to the conversation trying not to intrude on her conversation with what I assume are her friends. I hear the basic rundowns of their lives with Ava giving little to no responses. I was going to walk away until I hear. "so, you finally got the work done I, see? No longer Anorexic Ava." That I when I realize they are not friends at all. It's then that Ava makes eye contact with me. I take her expression as a sign to help her out, so I approach them and make my presence known. "There you are baby. I've looked all over for you. You were supposed to meet me up front almost twenty minutes ago."

"Well, aren't you going to introduce us Annie?"

asks the female. "Sorry. Amber, Craig, this is Darrius my bro..."

"Her boyfriend."

"Nice to meet you. We are old friends of Ava."

"Is that so. Funny she hasn't mentioned yall" I say. I look at the craig and notice he has his eyes trained on Ava's breast. "Ay my man are we going to have a problem. Keep your eyes on my woman's face not her tits alright?"

"My bad man I didn't mean any disrespect they just look real."

"Trust me my man they are real. Every time she rides me, I see how real they are. When I'm fucking her from behind grabbing them bitches, I feel how real they are. When I'm sucking on them until she cums, after she has had a long day, I taste how real are. You will never have to worry about my woman's body. I got that covered my dawg." I wrap my arm around Ava's waist and pull her into me and to sell the show I give her a peck on her lips. "Let's go baby. We have to get the place ready for movie night. "I would say nice meeting y'all, but my momma raised me to be honest." I let her go and continue pushing my basket. We finish shopping in peace and exit the store. As we are loading up my truck she yells. "What the hell was that back there? My boyfriend? You can taste how real? What were you thinking? I just wanted to make up an emergency not a whole fucking relationship. How will you explain this little show when it gets back to my mother because trust me it will get back to my mother."

"When that happens, I will take care of it."

"Sort of how you took care of this?" She storms off to her car across from me. "I'll meet you at your place." She gets into her car and flies out of the parking lot. I guess I'm not the only one affected by the feeling of her body against mine. When I get to my place Ava is already inside putting away groceries. I grab all the bags at once and bring them into the house. "Woman how did you get into my house?"

"I picked the lock. Where do you want this?" I Just stare at her waiting for further explanation. That doesn't' happen so I answer her question. "Just put it somewhere" I begin putting away the other groceries. I hear a loud thud and turn around. Ava is standing on the counter organizing he cabinets. "Are you crazy? Get down."

"Calm down. I'm not going to fall." She then

stumbles. I run to grab her ad she starts laughing. "You really thought I was going to fall." She says laughing. I suck my teeth and lightly tap her thigh. "Man, you play too much." I say. I walk back across the room. I hear another thud but think it's a can until I hear "Shit. That hurt." I turn around and Ava is on the ground holding her head. "See I told you to get down." I pick her up and place her on the island to look at her head. I see she has a small gash in her forehead. I walk to my bathroom and grab the first aid kit. "Next time you should listen."

"Last time I checked my daddy's name was Alexander not Darrius."

"You know you want me to be your daddy." She falters and I can see my response shocked her before she fakes annoyance. "Boy get out my face." She says laughing. I take an alcohol wipe and clean the blood from her wound. "Damn. Warn somebody before you do that shit."

"

Hush, you big baby." I finish cleaning it before drying and placing a bandage on it. Trying to be funny I kiss her bandage and say, "All better." The innocent gesture turned into a rush of blood to my dick. I pull away and reach to help her down.

Instead of placing her feet on the ground she wraps them around my waist and her arms around my neck. "Now make me get down." She taunts. I lean closer to her and whisper. "I have to shit."

"You are so nasty." She unwraps her legs and slides down my body. I quickly leave her in the kitchen and wait in the bathroom until the swelling goes down. Once everything is put away and I make dinner Ava suggests we actually have a movie night at her parent's home theater. I decide to shower and put on some lounge clothes. I drive over to their house and am met with the family leaving. "Hey, yall not coming to movie night?" They all start laughing. "What did I miss?"

"She got you." Arix says. I look at him confused. "Ava doesn't have a normal movie night. She starts the night with a good movie but as the night goes on it gets worse. Run while you can." I think he is joking until I look at his mother. She is shaking her head and shudders with fright. I start to turn around until Ava appears in the front door. "Darrius you made it." She says. I freeze and fake a smile. Her family laughs again and heads to their cars. "Hey so I guess it's just you and me."

"I guess it is." I try so hard to pay attention

to the movies but that went out the window the moment Ava's robe came undone. She has on nothing except a white lace bra and panty set. She then adjusts to sit on her feet, and I get a nice full few of her ass barely covered by her cheeky underwear. It doesn't help that the couple on the screen are making love. I spend the rest of the movie picturing myself in church willing my erection to go down. All of the movies have been sexually charged and I'm positive she did it on purpose. I'm not convinced that this movie isn't a porno. I close my eyes trying to block out the movie. At some point she curled up and place her barely covered ass right next to me. I figured out her game once she started making random noises and movements for me to look at her. I get up and get something to drink. She pauses the movie and follows me. grabbing my hand, she pulls me bk to the couch and climbs into my lap. "What is wrong with you?"

"What are you talking about?"

"I am basically naked. We have sent the past five hours watching movies that are basically porn and y you haven't even attempted to touch me. Why haven't you made a move? I know you want to fuck me."

"Are you sure about that?"

"I catch you staring at me when you don't think anyone is looking. I have heard you moaning my name in your sleep all summer and I felt your erection earlier when I jumped out of your arms earlier. If I wasn't sure, then the monster begging to be released underneath me is my answer."

"I think you are the sexiest woman I have ever seen Ava, but we can't."

"Why not we are both grown and single?" I don't mention that her brothers would kick my ass if I touched her in anyway other than platonic. "We just can't." I grab onto her waist to lift her of my lap, and she takes this as an opportunity to kiss me. I try to fight her until she bits my lip and I am completely gone. Her lips are way softer and thicker than they look. I pull her against me and deepen the kiss. She moans and pushes her center harder against me and I almost lose it. I turn laying her on the couch and look into her eyes. "Why are you so damn tempting?' I say before kissing her in her neck and down her chest. I rub my hands under her shirt and graze my thumbs against her ribs. I lower my hands until they brush against the top of her panties but before I can go any further our phones start ringing. I get up but it stops before I can answer. I put it back in my pocket and plan to finish what she started until I see her face. She looks like she seen a ghost. "Ava what's wrong baby girl? "Junior is in the hospital. They don't know if he'll make it, we have to go."

7

❦

Chapter Seven

Chapter Seven

Ava

I throw on a sweat suit and run -out of the house and quickly jump into my car. I knew this would happen one day. My worst fear came true. I quickly get to the airport and meet my parents at the jet. "Let's go." I don't have time to ask where they got a jet from, I plop down in a seat and pray that my brother will be ok. We arrive at the hospital and my mom quickly runs to reception "Alexander Moore please. I was told he was rushed here a couple hours ago." The lady looks at my mother then begins typing in her computer. "Yes ma'am, he is in surgery right now. I'll let his surgeon know you are here."

"Thank you." We are taken to the surgical waiting room and take seats. "I knew this would happen one day. God, please let my baby be ok." I watch as my mother unravels at the thought of losing her child. It then hits me I could lose my brother. As if he could sense my nerves, I receive a text from Darrius. Don't worry everything will be fine I hope so. I can't lose my brother. I just got him back. You won't lose your brother. In the short time I've known Junior I learned that it would take more than blowing him up to take him out I couldn't help but laugh at him. I didn't realize how loud I was until I looked up and saw my entire family looking at me like I was crazy. "Sorry, just thinking of that time Junior tried to crop dust me but ended up shitting himself."

"Oh my." My mother says laughing. "That boy completely ruined my carpet. I told him he tried that shit again he would be wearing a diaper all day long." We all burst out laughing remembering Junior's reaction. He was maybe sixteen at the time and we were rassling and Junior threw me to the floor and strained trying to fart in my face. He wound up shitting and having it run down his leg. We had shit running from the living room to the bathroom. As we are getting ourselves under control the doctor approaches us. "Are you all here for Sgt. Moore?"

"Yes. How does he doctor"?

"Well. He shattered the majority of his left leg, so we had to place multiple meatal rods in to aid in the healing process. Our main concern was the spinal injury. Luckily, it was not severed but it was severely damaged. I'm sorry to say he will likely never walk again." I made eye contact with my dad and we both knew what that meant. No more Marines. "He will be moved to ICU soon and then you may take turns visiting him." We all sit back down and wait. After what feels like hours, we are told we can see him. We agree that our parents should go first. However, my mom is not having it. "I can't. Ava, you go. I can't see my baby like that. I can't."

"Ok Momma I'll go." Me and my dad follow the nurse down the hall and are ushered into the room. I cross over the threshold and couldn't believe my eyes. My strong invincible brother looks so fragile.

His leg is lifted up and wrapped up to his hip. His face is covered in cuts and bruises. "Oh Junior."

Two weeks later

These last few weeks have been completely crazy. My mom spent these last couple weeks at the hospital with Junior. I have spent the last week locked in my room going over every bit of evidence gathered from Dianne's room. I have another check in with my team in a few hours and I feel like I have gotten nowhere. Without any notice Aiden bursts into my room. I hide the evidence as fast as I can. "Hey sis. Are you ok? You've been here way too long. My room is right next door, and I haven't seen you in three days."

"I'm working on a highly classified project. I am completely stuck. You need to go so I can finish."

"Fine, But tomorrow you and I are going to go out."

"Ok whatever." I really need my own place.

I gather the evidence and head out to meet my team. We reserved a conference room in town and completely took it over. "Please tell me someone has something."

"I might. This pen pal of hers may be the key." I rush over to Derrick and look at what he sees.

"See we originally thought it was like a virtual big brother big sister gig until I seen this." He hands me a printed email. I read through it and grin. *"I can't wait to hold you in my arms."* "How did I miss this. We have to find out who this is. He may have been grooming her." Maria, I need you to go back and ask her friends about this guy. Thomas put all the e-mails in order for me so I can get a story of these two. Put it in a PDF so I can read it. I'm going to rewatch the security footage. I'm trying to figure out how she got all the way to the street, and no one followed her." We keep looking until I realize she was followed. "Guys there is a guy just out of sight of every shot. I keep my eye on the guy and see that it's the driver. "New plan. Thomas, I need you to track down that van. I think it may be an uber. See if you can track down the van and the driver." My phone vibrates. "Alright y'all I gottta go but let me know if you find anything." It goes to voicemail before I can answer it. "Hello Miss Moore, this is Bethany Trescott with Miller Realty. I'm calling to let you know that I will be on site until five if you wanted to come take a walk through." I don't even finish the message. I grab my keys and head out the door. it isn't until I reach the house that I realize what I'm wearing. "Hello."

"Hi sweetie. My name is Bethany. Are your parents on the way?" She asks with a super fake smile on her face. I look at her in confusion. "Why do my parents need to be here?"

"Well sweetie you have to be eighteen to sign the paperwork and I doubt a job at McDonald's pays you enough to afford this mortgage." This happens every time my tattoos are covered I look at her and smile. I'm old enough to sign the papers trust me." I walk off and enter the house. "Ok. Well, this house has..." We walk the property and I'm not impressed. This isn't quite right. "I'm sorry. This just isn't it. " I then remember the sign I saw when I first came home. You have the forty-acre property outside of town, right?"

"Yes."

"I want it." What's the point to f me finding what I want when I can have it built?

"Ok well we can go check it out. "No. I don't need to. I want it. I don't think you have a house that fits my needs. How long for the papers to be drawn up?"

"With all due respect I don't think you can afford it."

"I can definitely afford it. I will give you five thousand over the asking price if I can get the papers by tomorrow. If that's a problem I can have one of the other agents handle the sale." My phone goes off with a message. I have to grab Mom's meds from Aiden before he goes to his game." If you'll excuse me. I have something to take care of. I leave before she can even understand what's going on.

How the hell do I end up in these situations? One minute I'm bringing Mom her meds the next I'm sitting in an interrogation room. I really don't have time for this. "I'll give you one last chance. Tell us who you are, or we will fingerprint and book for possession and intent to distribute. I knew you were trouble when you first came to town.

"I have told you already. I am Special Agent Ava Moore ad those pills are for my mom who is with my marine brother who is recovering from being blown up. my badge is sitting in my jacket pocket like I told you. Now If you still don't believe me run my prints. I am in the system." I hold out my hands and wiggle my fingers. "We will."

I am taken from the room where they scrub my

hands and check for fake prints. Then they take me to their printing system. I press my hand firmly and wait for them to run them through the system. After a few minutes, a notification rings from the computer. Hey uh chief you might wanna come take a look at this." I look at the officer with a smug look. "Well don't just stand there take the cuffs off her." They scramble to uncuff me. I place my hand in my pocket and show my badge. "This all could have been resolved at my car two hours ago had your officers listened. You also really need to get better at patting your suspects down." I reach to my thigh and pull out my gun. "I have been armed this entire time." The officer who arrested me turns completely pale. I approach him and whisper the next time you want to turn a search into foreplay make sure the other party isn't trained in martial arts." I then take his hand and turn until I hear something crack. "If you would excuse me now.my mother is waiting, and I have a case to close. Oh, and don't tell Antonio what you've learned today, and I won't file a complaint against this office." I am handed the medicine and escorted to my car. "I hop into my car and drive off. Fucking idiots. I drop mom the medicine and apologize telling her

I got stuck in the store on my way here. We talk for a while before I go back home.

I drop by Arix's room. He spends more time at home than on campus makes me wonder why he pays for a dorm. I don't see him, but I hear him in the bathroom. I sit at his desk and wait for him to come out. Me being the nosy person I am I dig on his desk. I pick up a binder and open it. "Untitled Series Reese Alexander." I flip through it and see that its plans for a new series by Reese Alexader. "What are you doing?"

"Sorry. I was being nosy. You know Reese Alexander?"

"You can say that." I look at the watermark of a sample chapter. "You are fucking kidding me. You're Reese Alexander."

"Shh tell the whole world why don't you."

"I'm sorry but that is so cool. I have read all of your books. Oh God. I've read all your books." I shudder in disgust as I remember the contents of his latest novel. "Wait gottta be making bank so why are mom and dad paying for everything?"

"How would I tell our parents that their twenty-year-old son is a millionaire because he writes porn?" I didn't think of that part. "I donate the amount of any large purchase to their company anonymously. So don't say anything "

"My lips are sealed." It looks like this family is filled with secrets.

8

Chapter Eight

Chapter Eight

Darrius

I 'm in so much trouble. In the last month since the movie night things with Ava have become interesting. Anytime we are near each other we find some reason to touch. Yesterday she sat next to me and "accidentally" sat in my lap. It was then I realized that she doesn't wear panties under her night clothes. There have been multiple times where we have almost been caught making out. Thankfully, we were able to play it off. We even sneak off to her construction site to make out like two teenagers.

"Hey Mr. Jones." Speaking of the devil. I look up and see Ava entering my office. "Hey, Ava. What you doing over here?"

"What can't I come check on a friend?"

"Your checking up on me usually leads to me beati ng my meat after you leave." She chuckles and lowers herself into my lap. "It's not my fault your lips taste so good. Come here." She pulls my face to her and presses her lips to mine I resist for half a second before I devour her lips. Just like always my manhood hardens and presses against my zipper. She feels me pressing against her and lowers her hand to my pants trying to pull it out. That's my cue to break the kiss. "We better stop before you get fucked on top this desk."

"That doesn't sound like a bad idea."

"It's not happening. We haven't even been on a date. I can't do that to you. I care too much about you and have too much respect for your brother to just fuck you. If we have sex, I want us to be in a relationship. It's what you deserve."

"You want to take me on a date fine. Tonight, at seven. You pick the place. Just a hint I can't stand sushi." She stands up and walks to the door. See ya later" Yep Arix is going to kill me. I go back to my work forgetting what I was going for a second. Locations. I continue searching through open storefronts. I decide to take a drive through the shopping district. I see a couple of places empty. I see one is having an open house. I pull over and decide to take a look inside. I walk inside ad can automatically see everything I can do with the place. I see everyone crowding around a little blonde chic. I wait for everyone to saunter away before approaching her. "Hello, my name is Darrius Jones."

"I'm not interested in whatever you're selling. Try the mall its usually pretty busy at this time." I laugh it off before continuing. "I actually wanted to ask if I could take a look upstairs assuming that that is included as well."

"Are you sure you want this place I mean the location alone makes this place out of most small business's price range."

"I'm far from a small business. Just show me upstairs."

"If you say so. Follow me." We make our way up the stairs, and I want it even more. "Up here is mostly empty like downstairs except it has a bar and a balcony."

"I'll take it."

"Very funny. How about you head to the mall? They have a couple spaces open. I think they would be better suited for you."

"What company do you work for?"

"Miller Real Estate." I search for the number and call it. "Hello, My name is Darrius Jones. I am here at one of your open houses I the business district. I would like to purchase the property."

"One of our agents should be onsite right now."

"Yes. I'm here with What's your name?"

"Bethany."

"Bethany. I'm here with Bethany and it doesn't seem like she understands how the process works. Can you get me in touch with another agent? I really need to close on the sale soon." \ "I'm sorry about the confusion. I will send another agent out there right now sir." \ "That's great." Not long after I end the call Bethany's phone rings. "Hello Sir. Yes sir. No, I understand it's just. Ok sir. Blake will be with you shortly" She then walks down the stairs and I follow behind her. "Excuse me everyone the place has been purchased. I have to ask you all to exit the building and tank you or your interest."

Once everyone is gone, she turns to me. "You better not be wasting our time."

"You are really sad. Had you asked you would know I plan to use this property to open my very well-known business's first physical store. I see you enjoy Daring Delights. Assuming the bra peeking from your shirt is any clue. By the blush in your face, I see my assumption is correct unlike yours." Before she can respond a man enters must be Blake. "Hello sir."

"How do you do? I'm Blake Miller owner of Miller Real Estate."

"Darrius Jones founder and CEO of Daring Delights adult novelty store." I glance in Bethany's direction and grin to see her chin practically on the floor. Damn that felt good. After dealing with the realtor, I decide to plan a nice evening for Ava. I make reservations at the only high-class res-taurant in town, Maria's. I then set up a romantic atmosphere in my sitting room. I throw rose petals on the floor leading to my bed, I place electric can-dles all around. I then place a couple condoms on the nightstand. I look at my watch and see I have fifteen minutes to get ready before I have to pick up Ava. I quickly change my clothes and brush my hair before spraying some cologne. I grab my keys and wallet and run out of the house. I stop by a flower shop and grab a bouquet of roses. While I'm driving, I get a call from Arix. "Hey man what happened to the place look like you fought valentine's day and lost." "If yo ass don't stop breaking into my place like that."

"Not breaking in if I own it remember."

"Anyway. I got a date. I'm on the way to get her now. I need to hurry so these flowers can get in some water. Did you know coriander meant lust?"

"No but I know what I'm buying my next girl."

"I'm at her house I'll call you tomorrow."

"Bet." He ends the call and I head to the house to get Ava. I'm guessing she chose seven because she knew no one would be home. "Ava. I'm here."

"Ok. Let me grab my purse." She enters the room and my heart stops. She looks gorgeous. She stands a couple inches taller in some killer black, red bottoms. She is also wearing a fitted one shoulder dress that hugs all of her curves. Especially her juicy ass. "Damn you look amazing." I look in her hand where she holds a medium sized bag. "Are you packing?"

"Is that even a question. My service weapon is

in my purse my personal weapon is strapped to my inner thigh. Why?"

"Give me your purse." She hands me the purse. I take her wallet and badge and place them in my suit pocket. I then place the purse on the sofa. "Let's go." I usher her out of the house and arm the house before closing and locking the door. We head to the restaurant and make it just in time for reservations. I asked for a secluded table so we wouldn't be interrupted. I allow Ava to sit first before sliding next to her. We order drinks and appetizers before we are left alone. We talk about pretty much everything on the sun our childhoods, jobs, and past relationships. I even know she wants a large family like she had growing up. The conversation paused when the food came. Once we finished, she scooted closer to me I assumed she was trying to be freaky until she leans over and whispers "We have to go." I look at her confused. "I'll tell you in the car, but I really need to get out of here. I nod then let her out the seat before paying the check and leaving a tip. As we are walking out, she pushes into me to hide her face. I lean down and whisper into her ear "Who are you hiding from?"

"The guy sitting alone by the door." I look up and see a bulky nicely dressed white dude. I commit his face to memory before walking out the door. I waste no time once we get in the car. "So, who was he?"

"An old friend from DC."

"If he was a friend, you wouldn't be hiding." I pull off and head to my house. "Fuck you."

"Now who is he for real?"

"It's a guy I used to know from DC."

"Why is he here? Is he the reason you trans-ferred out her? The reason is you are just now leaving your parents crib even though you could have been gone. Is he also the reason you're build-ing a fortress in the middle of nowhere?" I say referencing the massive eight-bedroom house with military grade security system. "You don't know what you are talking about."

"Judging by your reaction I know exactly what I'm talking about. I have listened to your brother talking about you constantly in the two and a half years I've known him. You are not the same person he described, and I think the Channing Tatum wanna be in there is the reason."

"His name is Taylor. He was my partner. He was

always really clingy I just brushed it off as a crush. Last year things got weird. He tied to kiss me after a rough case. I told him I didn't see him that way and he said he understood. I didn't believe him, so I asked for a new partner. After that I've had a couple accidents. I have been hospitalized three times in the past year. I was pushed down the stairs of my apartment, I was hit by a car, the last straw was when I got shot." I look at her in shock. "I was hit three times. My hips, knee and my chest. The bullet was two centimeters from killing me." I pull into my driveway and park. I then turn and face her. "He came to see me in the hospital the last time and told me I would never be safe without him." She then began to cry. "He was arrested but convinced the judge that I misunderstood him. They couldn't prove that he was my attacker, so the charges were dropped. No one believed the hot-headed federal agent who had lots of enemies. A week after the trail I was just getting home when I was hit in the back of the head. When I came to, I was in the hotel room tied to the bed. He spent the next ten days making small cuts across my entire body, feeding me just enough so I wouldn't starve. He wanted me to beg him to fuck me. I refused.

The last day he gave up and decided he wasn't going to wait any longer." She looks down and swallows another sob. Wrapping her arms around herself. "He ran and I put in to be transferred and here I am. I thought I could be safe here no one knew where I was from here, I made sure all of my personal files were marked confidential due to my undercover work. I guess he is a better detective than I thought." I get out and walk around the car pulling her into my arms. She lets the tears run free quickly socking my shirt. Her body shakes with agony "As long as I am here you are safe." I then carried her inside and placed her in my bed. I grabbed one of my shirts and a pair of my basketball shorts and handed them to her. She goes into the bathroom and takes a shower. I shower in the guest bathroom. When I get out, she is still in the shower, and I can hear her crying. I get in the bed and pretend to be on my phone. She comes next to me. "It's not the way I hoped but I did end the night with you in my bed."

"Shut up." We watch TV for the rest of the night in silence and I fall asleep with her wrapped in my arms. I say a silent prayer thanking the lord for bringing her into my life. I then pull her tighter into my side. I sleep better than I have in years.

9

Chapter Nine

Chapter Nine

Ava

It has been almost two weeks since my date with Darrius and I haven't seen him since. Thank goodness. I can't handle seeing him after my mini breakdown in his car. I can't stand the thought of what he thinks of me now. Thankfully, I have been busy with the final additions on my house. These past seven weeks have been so stressful. I have agents all over the state chasing leads to my case and the president has taken to calling me several times a day for updates. It really shouldn't bother me, but it does. There is something off about that man. I grab the last of my things and head down to meet my family. "Explain to me again why you just had to move out?" asks my dad. "Because Daddy, I'm almost 25 years old plus I have been on my own for six years. I have become used to doing as I please in my own house I need to get back to that."

"So, you needed a mansion to do as you please? Speaking of how the hell did you get three million dollars to build the damn thing?"

"We need to head out the contractor has another job to finish so if you want your keys," says Antonio. We load up in the cars and head across town to my house. I take the supervisor and my inspector on a final walk -through to ensure everything is in order. I sign off on the work, hand him the final payment, and he hands me my keys. I am officially a homeowner. I gesture for everyone to start unloading everything. My perfectionist assigned everyone to a room to unpack. I take my time organizing my master suite. I hear a knock on the door. "Come in but don't touch nothing."

"Can I touch you?" I hear from behind me. I refuse to turn around. Once he reaches m he tuns me to face him looking deep into my eyes. He then begins kissing my neck. "I thought our date went well all things considered." He says in between kisses. He rubs his hands down my thighs then up grabbing a tight hold on my ass. "Imagine my surprise when you ignore all my calls, don't reply to my text, and find every excuse to not be near me." he releases my ass before giving it a hard slap. He runs his hands underneath my shirt grazing my stomach.

"Because I was embarrassed. I cried on our first date. It wasn't even a pretty cry."

"You have nothing to be embarrassed about." He leans down and softly kisses my lips. He pulls me to his body and deepens the kiss. My nerves completely leave my body. Before I know it, he picks me up and places me in my freshly made bed. I eat to be mad at him for wrinkling my sheets, but I can't. not with his body pressed against my body. I can't do anything but ache for his touch. He kisses me down my body before taking off my sweatpants. "You are a strong woman who was failed by our supposed justice system. You have kept all this inside for long enough. I'm gonna help you let it go." He slides my panties off and settles between my legs. I go to remind him that my family is downstairs, but he licks up my slit and I lose all train of thought. I lay down and enjoy what he is doing to me. He is devouring me like I am his last meal. I rub my hands against his freshly cut head. He begins to lick my clit and I nearly break. I clench my legs together, but he spreads them apart and starts to suck my soul from my body. I push against his head because it feels too good. He wraps his arms around my thighs and pulls me harder against his face and goes to work. I can't hold back anymore I explode. He doesn't stop though he keeps going slurping all the juices flowing from inside me. I cum so hard this time my legs go numb. When my orgasm subsides, he pulls away and smiles. "Do you feel better now?"

"Fuck." I say. I spawl out in the bed. I feel him get out of the bed. I look forward to seeing what he is doing. He walks to the bathroom and comes back with a towel. He gras my legs and pulls me to him. I just lay there while he wipes me clean. "Put your pants back on. I'm sure your family is back with the pizza by now." I throw a pillow at him. This man is going to be the death of me. After the majority of my things are unpacked and put away my family heads out and leaves me to work. I turn on my computer and immediately get to work. I'm going through the reports given to me when I receive an email to my personal e-mail. I open and it's a video. In the video is a small room with a cot. It almost looks like a fancy jail cell. I almost turn it off thinking its spam until the camera flips and a masked man fills the screen. "Tell the president to resign and confess or his daughter will be sleeping for eternity." The video flips back and zooms in on the cot revealing a sleeping, Dianne. "Have a good day, Agent Moore."

"Shit." My theory about her just running away is now dead. I call the president and let him know what I have. "Do you know what he wants you to confess?"

"I have no idea. I haven't done anything."

"Are you sure? No matter how small or insignificant it may be. "

"Why the hell are you interrogating me when my daughter was kidnapped. How about you tell me why my daughter has been missing for two months and you haven't found a single lead. Stop wasting my time and find my daughter." He then hangs up. I look through every frame for a clue. I'm on my second pass when my phone rings. "Hello."

"Hey beautiful. What's wrong?"

"Hey Darrius. Just some stuff with my case." I almost give up for the day until I see a newspaper on the ground. I zoom in and clear up the image the best that I can. "Oh my God"

"What's wrong?"

"I got to go. I'll call you later." I know where she is. "Ok. Bye." I hang up and call my team. "I need all of you to drop what you're doing. She's in New Orleans. From the looks of the video, she is in some type of cell. Check all abandoned buildings and houses. Get back to me as soon as you find something." I can't wait to be released from desk duty. I got shot six months ago yet the department refuses to let me out into the field. They aren't sure I'm mentally ready to be back in the field. They wouldn't have to worry if that psycho bastard were in jail.

I go back to the images I captured to find any other clues in the video. There is a whiteboard in the background. On the board is a message. Trust no one Ava. I reply to the email. Tell me where she is. I can't do that. He needs to pay for what he did. I understand that but kidnapping his daughter isn't going to help you. She is safer with me than she is with him. Why do you say that did he hurt her? Tell me what happened. The truth will be revealed in time either by me or him. Tell me what you know I can help you. No. I have to get proof. I can't risk him getting away with his any longer. I go to reply but the account was deleted. I fall back into my chair in defeat. Then I get a text from a private number. Stop looking for her you are only making things worse. This will not end well. I try my best to my best to trace the e-mail and phone call, but he was smart.

I need to take a break. I decide to take a run. As I make my way around the neighborhood I feel as if I'm being watched. I slow a little to take in my surroundings. I hear the low hum of a motor running. I stop and pretend to tie my shoe while I look behind me to see a black van sitting in a driveway. I keep note of what it looks like in case I see it again. I recite the license plate in my head so I can run a check on it. I go back to my run and decide to lose my tail by jogging through the woods and taking a secret route back to my house.

Chapter Ten

Chapter Ten

Darrius

Today has been hell. Half of the contractor's team is out sick. I have been getting complaints because the community had discovered what I am opening. It's the 20th century for fucks sake. I decide to end the day early. I call Ava to see if she is up for hanging out. After going to voicemail three times with no text message. Somethings not right. I head to her house and buzz for her to open the gate. After no answer there I decide to let myself in. I park my car in the garage and search for the house for her. I enter her room ad I find out why she hasn't answered. This woman is completely knocked out. She didn't even make it under the covers. I pick her up and lay her under the covers before sliding in next to her. She made the plans for me we taking a nap. I pull her into me kiss her big ass forehead and fall asleep. The next thing I know is I feel wetness across my face. I keep pretending to be sleeping enjoying the kisses until I feel another one. "Did you just fucking lick me?" she dies laughing. "About time you woke up. What are you doing here and how did you get in?"

"I helped reset the security remember because you were scared a construction worker would break in Plus you didn't answer my calls or text, so I came make sure you were ok."

"So, you came in seen that I was fine and decided to take a nap in my bed with me in it?"

"You make it sound horrible. Like you're not my girl."

"So, I'm your girl now?"

"Would I be blowing up your phone if you weren't."

"I don't know, would you?"

"Stop playing with me woman." I pull her down

and tickle her until she I gasping for air laughing. I stop before stealing a kiss and jumping to my feet. "Come on. Let's get something to eat I'm starving."

"Motherfucker, if you don't stop walking around my house like it's yours." I keep walking as she follows behind me yelling. "Don't touch my kitchen!" I start looking through the fridge to see what she has. "Move. I got it. What you want?"

"Chocolate waffles and eggs."

"Ok." She washes her hands and gets to work. Watching her in the kitchen is like watching an artist. Everything is so smooth. I should have asked or something bigger just so I could watch her longer. "Here you go." She places my food down and I see my waffles are in the shape of a dick. I don't let it phase me. I cover the tip in whip cream and ate t really slowly. I look up to see her reaction and I'm not disappointed. "Do I need to leave yall alone?" I laugh and pick up the whip cream pretending to spray her. She grabs my hand causing me to press down covering her head in whip cream. "Oh shit. Baby I didn't mean to do that at all."

"Ok. That's what we doing." She stans up and walks to her pantry. When she comes back out, I take off running. She is now chasing me with a bottle of syrup. "I didn't mean to." Before I know it, she drenches me in syrup. We spend the nest thirty minutes coating each other in the stickiest foods we can find. Once we have run out of ammo we start cleaning up. Thankfully, both of us have good aims and most of the mess is on us. After we finish, I head upstairs and run her a bath. "Ava, I got your water ready." I quickly run to my car and grab my gym bag. I make my way to the guest room to shower. "Where are you going?"

"Take a shower."

"My tub is plenty big enough for the both of us." I look at her with a demonic smirk and chase her to the bathroom. We strip and ease our way into the tub. I pull her between my legs, and we relax "Did you honestly think we would wind up here after you tried to kill me?"

"I wasn't trying to kill you it was a warning shot. I wasn't aiming at you at all. And no, I didn't I figured that after my family came back, I thought wouldn't see you again." I soap up a towel and slowly wash all the sticky residue from her body. Once I have her thoroughly washed, she turns and washes me. I could fall asleep with how good his feels. I don't wat to bathe any other way again. She washes my face and I look her straight in the eye. "I feel like I have known you my whole life instead of three months." I take her lips into a soft kiss savoring this moment. This woman will be my wife. I pull into my lap making her straddle me. I kiss her deep and grind my dick against her pussy. Her shit is wet, and it is not because of the water. I slide into her and give her some slow deep strokes. I am just about to show out when she receives a notification. Siri then reads out "Aid says we outside."

"Shit." She jumps up ad my dick is greeted with the lukewarm water. She gets out of the tub and wraps herself in a robe. "You have to go my brothers are here."

"Which one?"

"All of them." I don't need to be told anything else. I drain the tub and rush to get dressed. She rushes downstairs to answer the door. While I find a place to hide. I then remember her security room. I grab my phone and keys and rush down the hall. I tur my phone to silent and sit and wait until they leave. I watch on the cameras as Ava opens the door. "Stop banging on my fucking door. I'm coming." She unlocks the door, and all four Moore brothers look at her with annoyance. "What took you so long?" Ask Junior. "Yeah," adds Aiden. "I mean your house is big but not that big."

"If yall must know I was in the tub."

"Already. Its only three o'clock." Says Arix. "Shut up and come in." They all come in. Tony pushing Junior inside "What are all of y'all doing here?" They all look around as if trying to find something. "We hadn't seen you in a couple of days, so we decided to check on you." Says Aiden. He then pulls the coat closet open. "I just seen all of y'all last night try again. Why are you opening my doors sir?"

"Junior." Urges Antonio. "I have this friend. She says she saw you walking out of Maria's a couple days ago and she also seen you and the same guy walking in the park yesterday." She does a great job of hiding her guilt. It was definitely us she saw. "I don't know what your friend saw but it wasn't me." I spent the day What does that have to do with my house?"

"We were seeing if you were hiding the dude in the house and that's what took you so long."

"Um hmm." Mutters Arix. "Can yall stop ganging up on me. Since yall are here help me clean up." I watch as each brother takes a room and pretends to clean only looking for me. Junior sticks to the living areas seeing as his wheelchair makes it hard for him to get through doorways. Aiden pretends to clean the kitchen while he fixes a monster sandwich. I see Junior meet him in the kitchen with my gym bag in hand. Shit. They whisper to each other then leave to go find the others I assume. Arix is in the laundry room taking clothes out of the dryer. My clothes. I forgot to take them out after our impromptu food fight. He grabs my shirt and walks down the hall meeting his brothers. "She has a man's stuff all over the house. This man has made himself comfortable in here. He ain't no one off."

"I peeked in the bathrooms and why was the toilet seat in her master was up. "

"So, he just left." Arix grabs the shirt. "Man, this looks mad familiar." He takes out his phone and starts typing. Shortly after my phone begins flashing. I decline the call and send him a text saying I'm in a meeting. Hey. What happened to that ugly ass shirt you bought from that old lady in Atlanta I think Ava stole it when her and mamma Randi brought me that soup last week while was sick. Ok "Its Dare's Ava was on her thief shit. She stealing his clothes just like she does ours."

"Ok the shirt is his but what about everything else?"

"Why don't we as Ava." They go into her bedroom where she is fixing her bed. "Uhm Micro, you got someone in our life and that we need to know about."

"Nope."

"So, you just have random dudes shit all over your house."

"He's not random."

"You just said no one was in your life."

"No. I meant you don't need to know about him. We are still kind of new and I don't need yall coming in and messing shit up for me. If yall are finished searching my house and raiding my fridge I would like to go take my nap. She walks them all to the door. And arms the security system. She looks up to the camera and says. I'll beat you to the jacuzzi. I look to the monitors and see that her brothers are gone the gate is closing behind them. I shoot off the backyard. When I get there Ava is already inside with her robe lying next to it. "Come on. We need to finish what we started in the tub before my brothers showed up". I strip and lower myself in fully prepared to show her what's up. "I guess I got to put you to sleep or else you'll be lying to our brothers."

Chapter Eleven

Chapter Eleven

Unknown

I take my time meticulously wrapping the gift and making sure nothing of mine falls onto the package. I carefully type out my message before attaching it. Happy Birthday Agent Moore, I thought I would be generous and give you a clue. The clue to finding me is closer than you think. I grab the gift and jump out of the bus. I approach her outer wall ad carefully scale he building watching to make sure no one can see me. I carefully hoist myself over the wall keeping my face hidden from the cameras I have spotted and avoiding the imbedded pieces of barbed wire she has hidden in the stones. This woman is clever. I quickly make my way to her front porch and place the present on the porch. I ring the doorbell and make my escape. I wait by the van and watch as she opens the door. She picks up the package and steps onto the porch looking around and trying to see who dropped it off. I wait until she walks back into the house before getting back in the van and driving off.

Ava

"This better not be a bomb." I quickly bring the package into the basement to my panic room. I open the box and instantly I'm confused inside is a birth certificate for a Diamonique Wilson born in Lafayette, Louisiana sixteen years ago. Along with it a picture of a woman in the hospital holding a newborn baby and the date is the same on the birth certificate. The last item in the box is a locket with a picture of the president and a woman who is not his wife. I add the contents to my evidence in my conference room. I head back to my room to finish getting ready to meet my family for cake and presents. I quickly throw something on before grabbing my keys and heading out. I arrive at my parent's house and quicky though my car into reverse unfortunately my mom is faster than I am and shuts the gate behind me. I continue up the riverway and put my car in the park. I stomp up the steps to a highly amused Aiden. What's wrong Ava changed your mind?" He asks throwing an arm around my shoulders. "I was told an intimate gathering with cake and presents not a house full of people I don't know."

"You haven't been home for you last six birthdays you really thought mom was going to let you get away with small. You must have forgotten who your momma is." We walk in and am bombarded with a jumble of "happy birthday."

"look how big you are" and "about time you come home." I wade through all the people before I find my mom fixing plates in the kitchen. "You have one hour and I leaving not a second over." Three hours later After opening all my gifts and eating myself sick of sweets I finally sneak off and head to my house. I jump into my giant tub. I allow all of my frustrations to wash away before getting out I dry ff and apply lotion. I decide against clothes before jumping into bed and taking a nap. I'm awakened from my nap by a rush of sensations.

I open my eyes to deep brown eyes and thick full lips latched onto my nipple. Seeing that I'm awake Darrius pulls away and smiles. "That woke you up. I have called your name and tapped you for nearly ten minutes. I got creative. Now get up." He demands before giving my nipples tender kisses and a tender caress of my pussy. "I'll give you more later." I follow him out of my bedroom. He turns back to look at me and realizes I'm still naked. "That's how we rolling I'm good with that." He then strips as he walks down the stairs. Now we are both walking through my house butt ass naked. "Negro what did I tell you about walking through my house like..." I can't finish my sentence after seeing what he has done. He recreated the ruined events of our first date. Candles and rose petals cover the floor surrounding a feast fit for a queen. I turn to Darrius who in now beside me "Thank you baby" I get on my tip toes and pull his mouth to mine showing him just how thankful I am. I break the kiss and settle to the floor. I reach for a bite before he swats my hand away. Taking the food and placing it into my mouth. I moan as the flavors hit my taste buds. I look into his lap and see that his dick is beginning to swell, and I decide I'm about to have the best birthday ever. Just as I swallow the last of the feast, I am yanked off the floor and pressed against his warm hard body. "You wanna tease people. I'll show you how to tease. He then crushes his mouth against mine and I a lost. I feel him carrying me, but I don't know where until I feel my back being pushed against a wall, he slides his hand between us and rubs my clit causing me to moan into his mouth. He lowers my legs for better access sliding two gloriously thick fingers into me. He continues to fuck me with his fingers and rub my clit until the pleasure builds up inside me. Just before it burst free, he pulls away from me placing me on the ground. "What the fuck?"

"I'm just playing the game you started." He then walks up to my bedroom. I follow him ready to curse him out until he suddenly turns and places sweet kisses down my neck. I am then picked up and thrown onto the bed. He looks down at me and is the first time that I have ever been scared of him. I can tell by his eyes I will not be walking correctly for a while. He lowers himself to me and slowly places kisses down my body. Before I can brace myself, he firmly and slowly licks my folds like an ice cream cone. He keeps working me over to the edge. Just like before when I'm ready to come he pulls away. "Motherfucker. If you don't ... holy shit." As I am telling him off, he enters me in one full thrust. I have never felt so full in my life. "Yeah, can't talk shit now huh." He says as he tears up my pussy. I can't even respond. I just squeeze his dick with my walls. "damn woman. Don't be doing that shit" He speeds up pounding into and my orgasm sneaks up on me and I burst with scream so loud I know will have me hoarse tomorrow. Just thinking he was down he pulls my legs up pressing my knees against my chest causing his strokes to go deeper. "Fuck yes." I try to meet him thrust for thrust for thrust, but he holds my hips down. I feel another orgasm rise I wrap my arms around him pulling him closer as I break digging my fingers into his back. Just as I find my release, he follows behind me. Emptying everything inside me. That's when I realize he wasn't wearing a condom. "You really shot up the club." He pulls out of me and walks to the bathroom coming back with a towel. "I sure did. You having all of my babies. "You just thought. Dude I take my birth control religiously." He lays back in the bed and pulls me to him covering us both up. "We gon see about that." The last thing I remember before sleep takes me is him kissing my check and whisper "Happy Birthday, baby."

Chapter Twelve

Chapter Twelve

Darrius

"I'm not sure what a child can tell us about running a business. What could she possibly know about being a vice president?"

"Can you shut the fuck up and listen for once. Last time I checked I don't need anyone's approval on who I put in what position." I yell to the poor excuse of a man on my computer screen. "Aaliyah you can continue." I then wait for her to continue her presentation on the changes she would like to implement. I hear Ava moving around on the bed behind me. I keep my composure even though I want to put the erection that is rising to good use. I didn't realize I zoned out until I could hear Arix calling my name. "Damn man where you were?"

"Sorry ya'll I have a couple things on my mind."

"Let me guess it has something to do with the lump that just got out of your bed." I slowly tilted my screen down to ensure he couldn't see her face. "Mind your business. When will the first book be ready for our launch?"

"The rough draft is done. I just have a couple touch ups and it's headed to the printers. I say like six weeks. They should be in your hands for packaging."

"Great." Ava walks behind me and rubbing her hand across my cheek s she passes heading into the bathroom. I am so thankful my bed is on a platform causing her head to be cutoff in the video feed. "Ok so we will start advertising the new deals and allowing pre-orders now. Its nasty right?" I address to Arix. "Now who ain't listening." Arix snaps back and looks at me still deep in thought. "I'm sorry Bro. Is that everything?"

"Yeah. Everyone, enjoy the rest of your holiday. I'm sorry for cutting in on your family time.

Happy Thanksgiving. See you all in the office Tuesday Morning." I end the call wondering what is up with Arix." I close my computer and head to Join Ava in the shower. I strip my clothes and open the door sliding in behind her. I wrap my arms around her and let out a pained hiss when I feel the water against my skin. "Goddamn woman you trying to cook in here."

"That's what you get. Ain't nobody told you to get your ass in here with me."

"Yes, Somebody did."

"Who? Surely wasn't me."

"My dick." Her response was a swift punch to my stomach. "Keep hitting me. I got something for abusive women."

"What you gon do. Nothing." Before she could even blink, I grab her turned her around and pressed her back into the wall slightly liftin her and impaling her on my dick."

"Fuck." She grunts wrapping her legs around waist. "Can't talk shit now huh. Keep beating on me and I'm gon beat this pussy loose." I gently pull out before hammering back into her. I forcefully thrust into her until I feel her walls tighten round me. "Nah. You can't come yet." I pull out before she can reach her climax. I lower her to the ground, then turn to wash myself clean. "I know fucking not. If you don't get your ass over here and let me bust on that dick."

"Nah. you don't get the satisfaction until you learn to keep your hands to yourself. Hurry up and wash off. We have to be at your parents' house in an hour meaning you need to be getting dressed now." I rinse and step out of the shower. I walk into my closet deciding what to wear "See ya later."

"You leaving?"

"Uh does it look like I have thanksgiving clothes here?"

"True."

"Am I meeting you at your place tonight?"

"That depends on if you still gon be playing games later."

"I'm not playing games. I'm showing you what happens when you start beating on me like a man. I don't fuck men. I surely don't make them come. Until you learn to keep your hands to yourself you ain't getting none of this." She doesn't respond just stomps out of my house. I can't help but laugh at her tantrum. I stop laughing when I hear her car pull off entirely too fast. I pick up my phone and shoot her a text. Slow the fuck down. You are not my daddy According to you the other night I'm big daddy of did you forget. I get a middle finger salute as a response. I throw my phone on the bed as I lotion down and put on my clothes. I decide to dress it up with a gold chain, diamond studs, and I switch out my apple watch for the new Rolex I bought for any early birthday present to me. I am brushing my hair when I hear my phone go off. If you don't bring your ass here. Ava fashionably late ass beat you here. You can't get a plate until I'm there huh? Yep. Now bring your ass. I grab my keys and make my way to the Moores.' I walk into the door and Arix walks to greet me before stopping dead in his tracks. "What the hell? You and Ava got dressed together today?" I am confused until Ava walks out of the kitchen and see wat he means. Other than the fact Ava has rips in her jeans, and her timbs are heels were dressed the same. She even has the same gold chain as me. "Don't hate because we know how to dress little bro." clowns Ava. I dap up Ree before side hugging Ava trying not to linger too long even though I want to keep her pressed against me. "Where ma at?" I ask. From the moment Arix introduced us

Miranda Moore has insisted I call her Ma. She said she could already tell I was going to be family. "Her and Junio are setting the table." I walk in the kitchen and see that with Ma Miranda and Junior is a tall brownskin standing really close to Junior. "Happy Thanksgiving," I say in greeting. They all return my greeting. I press a kiss against the feisty older woman before shaking heads with Junior. Surprised to see the man that is supposed to be paralyzed standing with the help of braces and a walker. I then turn to the mystery guess and introducing myself. "Hello gorgeous. I'm Darrius Jones, but everyone calls me Dare. Well except Ava. I'm a friend of Arix' "Payge Roberts, I'm Ava's best friend. "Nice to meet you." I grab her hand and place a kiss to her knuckles "You as well." She replies. "Alright that's enough." Interrupts Junior. "I'm sorry. This you Junior?"

"Nah that's like my sister. I just don't need you breaking her heart with your LA charm." She must not have liked that answer because she made a quick exit without saying a word. I wonder if Ava knows her brother is fucking her best friend. "No worries s, man. I have a lady. You look though bro. Soon you'll be. Back on the court taking them L's."

"Negro please." Before we can continue our conversation everyone files into the room ready to eat. We all take our seats and dig in. After Dinner and the football game. Everyone goes their separate ways. I head to my house and place my car in the yard before packing a bag and taking a short run to Ava's house. I use the back gate, so no one sees me. I decide this sis the last time we will be sneaking around I'm telling Arix. When I get into the house I am met with a very sexy view. Ava is clad in so-called lingerie. The set is a bunch of straps crossing perfectly to conceal her nipples and the apex of her thighs. "Is this your way of apologizing or are you hoping I will forget that you're on punishment."

"I can't promise I won't hit you anymore, but I will keep my hands to myself." I approach her. "You will keep your hands to yourself, or this shit here is over. I will not spend the rest of my life being someone's verbal and physical punching bag. I don't care how much I love them?"

"So, you love me?"

"Maybe, I guess you will have to wait for me to tell you." I grab her face a firmly press my lips against hers. I lower my hands and wrap them around her waist pulling her into me. Deepening the kiss. I pull her up and carry her to her bedroom. I place her at the end of the bed and slowly undress teasing her. I strip down to my boxers saving the best for last. I lean towards her gently pushing her to lay on the bed. I slide the strips of fabric of her body and enjoy the heated gaze she gives me. I follow the fabric down her body kissing each inch as it is revealed to me. Once I near her opening, I softly blow on it causing her to tense at the cool breeze. I then flatten my tongue and drag it firmly against her as she pushes against me trying to increase the pressure. I lick even harder as she starts leaking. I devour her like she is my favorite ice cream and its melting, As she nears her orgasm, she begins to tighten her thighs against my ears. I stop before she can come and release the hold she has on my head. She begins to squirm on the bed begging for release. I stand and slowly lower my boxers showing her exactly how much I want her. Once I am completely naked, I climb onto the bed hovering above her. I grab her left leg and slowly thrust into her letting her feel every inch as it spreads her hot tight walls. "fuuuuuuck." She grunts as I bottom out. "Yeah. You see how good it feels to be when your good for Daddy." I continue to thrust slowly making my point. "You don't have to be defensive against me. I will only hurt you when you ask for it." I push her knees into her chest allowing myself to reach deeper inside of her. I begin to speed up and rub my thumb against her clit urging her to climax. "YESSS!" she screams fisting the sheets and spasming so hard she early pushes my dick out. My orgasm sneaks up on my causing me to sloppily slam into her filling her completely with my cum. I lay on the bed and pull her on top of me. We fall into ecstasy induced sleep.

13

Chapter Thirteen

Chapter Thirteen

Ava I will kick Arix's ass. My brother has been avoiding me for the past month. I stand in the mirror seething a how mad I am even when I was in DC, we spoke at least twice a week. I inspect my outfit and battling with the decision to change or keep this on. My mom wants tonight to be a formal dinner, so I went with a white floor-length gown covered in shimmer and form fitting. My favorite part is the slits up both legs. I look at the time and realize I don't have time to change. I rush out the door and head to my parents' house. When

I arrive, everyone is Already there. I make my way into the house and the first thing I hear s Aunt Kat yelling "That heifer always late. I have time to starve to death before she gets here."

"Damn Auntie. That's how you do me?"

"If you would learn how to use a watch I wouldn't have to."

"Alright fair enough. I'm sorry yall I couldn't decide which dress to wear."

"That means you have multiple prom dresses in your closet?" asks Junior. "Yes. I have them from weddings I have been to these last couple of years."

"Ok. So, the princess has arrived can we eat now."

"Not until we take pictures." Everyone lets out a groan knowing my mom can spend hours taking pictures. An hour later I finally get to sneak away to use the bathroom. As I am washing my hands, I hear a knock on the door. "One second, I'm almost done. I dry my hands and open the door. Before I can exit, I am pushed ack into the room ad pressed against the sink. I look up and come face to face with Darrius. "I haven't touched you in three days. I'm ready to combust." He smashes his lips into mine and forces his tongue into my mouth. I waste no time in reciprocating. It feels like we're fucking with our tongues. Entirely too soon he pulls away. "I promise baby after we tell everyone, and dinner is over I will take you home and fuck up your life." I can feel he wants to say more but stops himself and leaves me in the bathroom. I get myself together before leaving the room. Once I rejoin everyone, we spend another hour taking pictures. Thank God she invested in a small steam table because I was not waiting in line to warm up my plate. Once my plate is loaded up, I plop myself at the table and am about to dig in before I feel a hard smack against my hand. "You know we say grace in this house. The hell is wrong with you child." Fusses my mother. I put my fork down and rub my stinging hand. I swear I think she bruised my hand. After everyone has finally sat down and we say grace I shovel food into my mouth. I haven't eaten all day to make room for everything. I don't stop until I hear everyone laughing. "What's so funny?"

"You. Looking like a damn cartoon character." Mocks Junior. "I was starving."

"We can tell." Laughs Aiden. I stick my tongue at him and continue eating my food. After my plate is cleaned, I sit back and wait for my mom to serve the chocolate cake. As we wait, we all catch each other up on what's been going on in our lives. The conversation shifts to the topic of one of Arix's classmates being pregnant. "Speaking of pregnancies when are you going to give us a baby Ava?" asks Antonio. My dad spits his drink on the table. "Hold up now my baby too young to be pregnant."

"Dad she is twenty-five."

"And you're twenty-eight where is your baby?" he doesn't answer just puts his head down. We all know it will be a miracle for Tony to have a baby. I am glad when my mom comes back with the cake. As we enjoy the doorbell rings. My mom runs to answer it. When she comes back, I am shocked to see the director of the FBI follow my mom into the dining room. I'm busted. "Everyone this is Director Lewis Of the FBI."

"Hello Everyone, I'm sorry to bother you but I have urgent news to speak with Agent Moore about." I wince when he says Agent. "Yeah, right like Ava could be an agent." Says Antonio. Everyone laughs except me and the Director. It's when they realize I'm not laughing they know he isn't lying. "You told us you were a business consultant when did you become an agent?" My father asks as he rounds the table to speak with us. Director Lewis looks between us confused. "I will explain later right now I need to talk to my boss in private." I lead him into the kitchen. "What I so important that you interrupted my family's Christmas dinner?"

"We got an anonymous tip that the president engages in illegal activity, and it may have to do with his daughters disappearance. We also think we have a mole in our department."

"How do you want me to move forward with the case?"

"Anything that is not already in the system remains that way. I don't want anyone outside of your team briefed on the case. Not me. Not the parents. I want this girl found unharmed. "Yes. Sir."

"Enjoy the rest of your holiday. Sorry for outing you to your family. A word of advice, my grandmother always told me what's done in the dark comes to the light. You should really talk to your family about the real reason you came back home."

"Yeah, I see that. I know I should talk to them I just don't really know how."

"Hopefully on a good note." We exchange

pleasantries and I walk him to the door before slowly joining my family in the living room. "Would you like to explain first, or should I just start cussing you out?"

"See that right there is why I didn't tell you. Y'all freak out about nothing. Junior has been in the Marines for ten years and y'all are proud of him, but when I try to serve my country it's a problem."

"It's different because you're not six foot and over two hundred pounds."

"Yes, but I am also one of the best shots in the bureau. Trust me the shit I've been through proves..." I stop mid-sentence when I realize what I've said. "What the fuck do you mean the shit you've been through?!" God dammit I guess it's time to let the cats out of the bag.

Chapter Fourteen

Chapter Fourteen

Darrius I watch as Ava's family waits for her to answer her mother. "It means that I was not forced to transfer I requested it for my safety." I tell them about my troubles with Taylor and my decision to leave. "Babygirl, you know you could have told us we would have gotten there by any means necessary."

"Yeah, judging by this house and all of your trips I guess business is doing better than I thought. What did you finally take Ronald up on his offer" She basically spits. Mentioning the biggest drug dealer in town. According to Ree he has been propositioning Mr. Moore for years about washing his money through Moore Industries. "How dare you accuse us of such a thing. As you must know, me and your mother have finally signed a major contract that was quite profitable. So no, our recently acquired wealth has nothing to do with shady dealings. It's because me and your mother busted our asses to make sure that we have something to leave our children but judging by that fort you had built I don't think you need it too much."

"Yeah A, I heard from some of the crew that place had to run you a couple million dollars? I know the Feds don't pay you that much." Says Tony. I have also wondered how she afforded the house. We all turn to her waiting on an answer. "School. I earned almost three million dollars in scholarships and grants. I only used a portion of it. The rest I split between savings and investments. At this point in time, I could quit and never have to work another day in my life if I wanted to. Since I'm made to be the bad guy why don't y'all ask Arix just how he is actually putting himself through school." This isn't going to be good. Arix told his parents that he was awarded a grant by a publishing company after he won a short story contest. In reality he signed a book deal and has been using that to fund his education. "What is she talking about Aix."

"I'm Reese Alexander." Momma Randi looks like she is going to faint. I assume she knows exactly who that is. Everyone starts arguing back and forth about how family shouldn't keep secrets. I can see that Ava is getting worked up so without thinking I pull her into me. I run my hands up and down her arms before placing kiss to her temple. he room goes dead silent. I look up and realize the situation. "Why the hell are you touching on her like that?" I freeze before looking to Arix. I can tell by his eyes that he wants to know the same thing "So, I wasn't tripping. You are fucking him?" ask Arix. "Arix!" chastises our mother. "Nah Ma. I thought something was up, but I chalked it up to me just being overprotective of A, because I know my boy wouldn't go behind my back and do exactly what I asked him not to do." He walks up to me and balls his fist. "Arix it's not like that."

"

Let me guess she was the woman you bought them flowers for. You're also the dude that left the clothes in her dryer. I thought it was a coincidence until we had that meeting." I think of the conference and I'm positive that her head was out of frame. "I knew that I recognized the tattoo, but I couldn't place it. Until tonight. Few people have a cheetah surrounded by roses on their thigh." He the reaches for the slit on Ava's dress revealing the tattoo. "How could you man? Out of all the people you choose my sister."

"It just happened. And I didn't betray you. I was already feeling her before you told me to leave her alone." Ava shimmies out of my arms and approaches her little brother. "You told him to leave me alone? Who the hell do you think you are dictating who I can and cannot date?" She gets yells jamming her finger into his chest. "He's not good for you." Interrupts Antonio. "The man makes porn or a living for Christ sakes. He nowhere near the type of man you should be with."

"Yeah, Ree told us how he treats women. You know he is sleeping with a barely legal employee of his. He even gave her a promotion to keep her quiet." I feel my blood boil. "Is that really what you think of me? That I am so down bad I would sleep with a child. How about we stop making assumptions and look at the man who beat two men half to death without breaking a sweat. I hear the case is still open. I'm sure Lafayette Police department would love to receive a tip on your whereabouts. You can sit in prison and rot while I spend my days burying my dick deep in your sister's tight ass pussy. As soon as the words fully leave my mouth, I feel an intense pain across my jaw. I place my hand against my cheek soothing the ache before throwing my own punch and landing it causing Arix to stumble a bit. He quickly recovers and lunges at me hurling us to the ground. We exchange blows for a while before Junior and Tony jump in for what I assumed was to break us up until I feel a swift kick to my side as Arix lays underneath me. I topple over in pain and have just enough time to steady my breathing before another one is delivered to my other side. I keep fighting trying to protect myself as I look around for Ava who I see yelling at us to stop. I can feel myself weakening and a fog taking over. Before it's too late I yell out. "Ava, I love you." I then relax and let the darkness consume me. I come to a little bit later and fell myself moving. I open my eyes to see Arix, Junior, And Antonio being loaded into cop cars as I am being lifted into an ambulance. I hear my name and look over to see Ava with tears running down her face. The last thing I hear before I return to the darkness is "I'm right here baby. Don't worry everything will be okay." "We're losing him. Step back ma'am." A mask is placed over my nose. Just before darkness takes me.

Chapter Fifteen

Chapter Fifteen

Ava I sit in the chair and watch as doctors and nurse rush through tending to patients. I wait for the nurse to return and give me an update on Darrius. I was told they lost him twice but were able to bring him back. "Family of Darrius Jones."

"Hi. I'm Ava Moore, His fiancé, is he going to be, ok? "He is still in surgery right now. He has several broken ribs, a collapsed lung a broken jaw, several bruised ribs, a fractured hand and swelling of his brain. The doctors are doing everything they can to help him, but it's up in the air at the moment. I'll come back later to give you an update." She walks off leaving me alone with my parents in the waiting room. "He will be ok honey. God has his hands on him. Why don't you go home and change, and we'll call you with any updates." I look down at myself and realized that my dress is covered in Dare's blood. Seeing this just pisses me off more. I hide my anger and turn to my mother. "I hope so ma. No sense in me sitting here stressing. I'm gonna stop by my house really quick and shower and eat something. Call as soon as y'all hear anything."

"We will baby." I grab my phone and call Payge to come get me. She gets here pretty quickly "Girl what the hell is going on with the Moore's? Who in the hospital?"

"Darrius is. After my hot-headed brothers beat him to within an inch of his life."

"What did he do?"

"Fucked me."

"Girl, stop playing."

"I'm not joking. They tried to kill him because we were fucking ""The hell is wrong with them?"

"Apparently, they like to solve problems by beating it to a pulp. Which is why I'm going to have a little talk with all three of them." We pull up to my house and I open the gate from my phone. "Ava. I know we haven't really spoken over the years, but I'd like to think I still know you. So, I know I can't change your mind or stop you from doing anything reckless. I just want yo to be careful. Don't do anything that could ruin your life and chance at being happy." I get out of the car letting what she said sink in. I quickly shower change and fix myself a sandwich before gathering my things and heading to the police station. "I' m Special Agent Ava Moore ad I need All three of my brothers in interrogation for questioning."

"I'm sorry but I can't do that."

"You can or I will have my boss take them into federal custody your choice." I wait as she calls over a fellow officer and they escort me into a room. I wait a few minutes before the door opens and my brothers are ushered inside. Unfortunately for them it's a holiday and a weekend so they won't see a judge until Monday. "You can uncuff them trust me they won't hurt me." The officer releases them and leaves the room. Before either of them can even think to say something, I kick Arix who is the closest to me in the chest causing him to bend over I use that moment to force my elbow into his jaw. I then unholster my gun and pistol whip junior busting his lip. Tony is the easiest I send all my strength in my foot straight to his balls. Recovered Arix hurls towards me preparing to restrain me. I then use his momentum to lay him out on his back. "Don't yall remember, I am trained at this shit. I have as much experience as mister marine. Come on yall like to jump people come on try that shit on me."

"We aren't fighting you, Ava."

"That's because yall are some bitches."

"You're our sister."

"Not anymore. I have one brother. He didn't let his brotherly instincts takeover and nearly kill someone." I'm tired of talking. I attack swing and kicking at all three men they try their hardest to restrain me. I backed out when I come back to myself. My arms are crossed over my chest and I'm being bear hugged from behind. I assume it is one of my brothers until I see they are bloody and unconscious on the floor. 'I thought you said they were your brothers?"

"They were now they are just my momma's sons. I walk out of the room still pissed ad now heartbroken. I refuse to let anyone feel they have control over my life, not even my family. I head to the front desk and ask that the charges be dropped. After washing my hands and icing them. I head to my office and grab my case file before going back to the hospital. When I arrive, he is in recovery and will be moved to his room soon. I sit in the waiting room going over my notes. It's not until I look at the birth certificate that I realize something is up. I pull up Dianne's birth certificate and am shocked at what I see. It's fake. I go to the DC Birth records and realize that there is no Dianne Williams born in DC on November 7, 2008. However, Diamonique Wilson was born in Baton Rouge, Louisiana on November 7, 2006. I run their Social Security Numbers and see that Diamonique is reported missing just two months before Dianne shows up. Ten years ago. He moved to Maryland and changed his daughters name and her age. I look up her school records. She is a senior. How if they have her as fifteen? I keep scanning and see she was "skipped" ahead twice. Dianne Williams is actually Diamonique Wilson. How is it that this poor girl was kidnapped twice? "Ava?" I look up and see Darrius's nurse. "He can have visitors now." I quickly grab my things and follow her down the hall. When I enter, I want to cry. He is hooked to so many machines. I approach his bed and take his hand not mine. "They have him in a medical induced coma due to the swelling in his brain. They will take him off within the next couple days depending on how he responds to the test and medications. All he needs to worry about is making it through the night." Says the doctor. I didn't realize he was standing there. "I'll be back later to check in on him. Let the nurse know if you need anything. I sit on the sofa next to his bed. I sit unmoving until my mom walks in. "Ava baby you need to eat."

"I'm not hungry. "

"I don't care eat something."

"It's all my fault."

"What are you talking about Ava."

"My attack. Dare being here. The case."

"That is not your fault Ava. You're just going through a rough time baby."

"Dare didn't feel comfortable being with me because of Arix, but I didn't listen, and I wouldn't take no for an answer. Now he could die because of me. A child has been missing for four months because I have been too caught up in my personal life to look closely at the evidence. He attacked me because I just laughed at his advances and weird behavior. Had I shut it down he wouldn't have taken me. I wouldn't have had to endure the next three days of agonizing pain and having his disgusting body inside mine. I wouldn't have had to suffer through the pain of losing that monsters baby. I didn't care how I got her. I wanted a baby. Why couldn't I have my baby, momma." My phone vibrates. Alerting me to a message. It's probably my team with an update. I read the message and it's as if time freezes. I let the phone slide out of my hand. "NO!" I scream at the top of my lungs not caring where I am. I hear footsteps rushing into the room. "What's going on?" I hear. I feel arms wrap around me and someone calling my name. "She's dead."

"Who Ava who's dead.?"

"Dianne.

16

Chapter Sixteen

Chapter Sixteen

Darrius

I smell bacon. I open my eyes and I'm in Ava's bedroom. I look to my side and see her spot is empty. I remove the covers and stand to my feet. I'm in my pajamas. Ava never lets me sleepover. She is too scared of her brothers showing up again. I make my way downstairs following my nose to the food I smell cooking. I turn into the kitchen and am shocked at the sight. "Daddy!" two small boys run towards me and cling to my leg. "Morning baby. I told you to stop working so late. You need to rest." Ava turns to me, and I'm shocked to see that she's very pregnant. I rush to her and grab the plates from her. "You do this every time. I'm pregnant not cripple. I can cook and feed my children. Go set the boys up at the table please." I place a kiss on her forehead before chasing the boys through the kitchen and placing them in their highchairs. We enjoy our breakfast and make plans to go to the park and hold the baby alligator. Once we are all dressed and ready, we head out. we get to the park and the boys shoot off like torpedoes. "Slow down boys." They turn and run back to me. We check in and the boys run to the alligator enclosure. As the associate tends to the boys Ava and I sit on the bench. "If anyone had told me that I would be a wife and mother to four little boys I would have told them not to wish that on me. I wouldn't ask for anything else. Except maybe a little girl."

"well after these get here maybe we can try for one."

"Five kids though Dare."

"Hey, we can have as many kids as you want. It's not like we can't care for them we just need to find a nanny for when you decide to go back to work."

"You are the best husband and father you know that right? Please wake up."

"What?"

"Ava needs you wake up." I look confused before everything disappears, and I'm plunged into darkness. "He should have woken up by now. Why is he still asleep?" I hear Momma Randi ask. "He is completely fine physically. He could be just exhausted. His body needs to recuperate from the damage." I am pulled back to Ava's house. We are in the living room. The two boys from before are older and sitting in the floor watching T.V. I am flanked by two identical boys and holding an infant boy. I guess I don't make girls. "I got popcorn!" Yells Ava as she enters the room. The boys rush to her grabbing a bag before going back to their seats. I swear I have a heart attack when I realize she is pregnant again. I look down at the boy in my arms who is not even one, yet she is looking ready to pop. "Y'all little sister must want some popcorn too she has decided to use my ribs as a punching bag." Or maybe I do.

I need a vasectomy. We watch movies until the boys fall asleep. I take each one and bring them to their beds. When I get back in the living room Ava is also knocked out. I pick her up and bring her to our room. Once she is settled, I climb in behind her and wrap my arms around her and our baby. I return to the darkness and voices. "Ava is still out of it, but she is awake. I just wish Dare would wake up. He could snap her out of it." Says Mr. Moore "I'm scared baby. You heard the therapist. Some people never return from breaks like that."

"She'll be okay baby. They both will." What is wrong with Ava? I try to ask but my lips feel too heavy to open. What is going on? I am pulled back into my dreams. I am alone in the house and it's a mess. like someone trashed it. I search through the house for my family. The boys rooms are tossed about but empty. Our family photos are destroyed. I peep in the nursery and our baby girl is lying in her crib hidden under blankets and toys fast asleep. I pick her up and cradle her to my chest continuing to search for my wife. When I turn to exit the room, I notice feet poking out of the closet. I open the door more and am haunted by the sight. My boys were tied up with tears running down their faces. Ava laying in a pool oof her blood. "No!" I scream and am pushed out of the dream.

I open my eyes to bright lights and blurred

faces. I blink a couple times and come face to face with a doctor. "Hello Mr. Jones. I'm Dr. Arceneaux. You're alright. I'm need you to relax your throat so we can take the tube out." I relax and feel the uncomfortable pressure as the tube leaves my throat. I am handed water and I take a couple sips before attempting to talk. "What happened?" I ask. I have flashes of fist flying at me. "Was I robbed?" I look at the faces around the room. Momma Randi looks pissed I think its t me at first until I see Junior, Arix and Tony looking guilty and bruised up. Aiden is in the corner looking funny. What is going on I wonder.

"Would you three bitch asses want to tell him why he is here or should I." Growls Momma Randi.

"We're sorry man. We were just so mad. We just want what's best for our sister." I look at him confused. "Arix made it seem like you were some fuckboys who didn't care about women's feelings. So, we agreed that you needed to stay away from our sister. Then Arix said he thinks yall were dating behind our back we told him you wouldn't betray him like that especially after he threatened you." Says Tony.

"Yeah. We thought it was really grimy of you

if you were really messing with our sister without talking to Arix first." Says Junior.

"You're a playboy we both know it. I didn't want my sister to be just another body. I could see that y'all were feeling each other but, I let them make me think I was crazy when I was right all along. I was mad that you were fucking my sister after I asked you not to. So, my anger at you and at myself for ignoring it just boiled over. I blacked out. I didn't realize what I was doing until I was being pulled off you."

"You mean to tell me that you couldn't trust me your best friend to take care of your sister so you dogged me out to your brothers and then nearly killed me because I wouldn't allow you to dictate my relationship with your sister."

"I know it sounds stupid, but I was angry. I wasn't trying to kill you."

"And you two didn't even bother to get to know me first you just went along with what he said?"

"We didn't think we needed to. Arix is your dog. We never thought to question him. He made it seem like Ava was just a challenge to you."

"Would open an adult store in the bible belt for a challenge?" I grab my wallet of the nightstand.

"Would I uproot my life for a challenge. Would I buy this for a challenge?' I shove the recently purchased engagement ring into their faces. I love that woman with every breath in me and you tried to ruin that. Get out." I force my voice to remain calm. "I'm sorry D. if I knew how you felt about her, I would have never interfered. "YOU DIDN'T FUCKING ASK!" I scream. "I kept it from you to give you a chance to see Ava and I as friends hoping you would soften to the idea of us being together. Instead, it made it worse so I'm sorry for keeping it from you, but I will never be sorry for loving her. As far as I'm concerned you and I are just business partners. Please leave. All of you." I watch as all three men exit the room. The one person in my life that I thought I could trust besides Ava nearly killed me. Guess we didn't know each other like we thought. "I'm so sorry son." says Mr. Moore. "I didn't raise any of them to be violent. I can tell you really care for my daughter."

"It's not on you. Mr. Moore and I love your daughter very much sir."

"Call me pop. I have a feeling you aren't going anywhere anytime soon."

"No. I'm not." It's then that I realize the reason

I'm here in the first place is nowhere to be found. "Where's Ava?"

"She felt guilty. You were touch and go. She lost her baby this time last year. Then she found out her victim is dead she couldn't take it she broke. There is nothing they can do here so they sent her home. She hasn't left the bed except to use the bathroom. We're worried Dare it isn't good. "Bring me to my wife. Now."

Chapter Seventeen

Chapter Seventeen

Ava

It's all my fault It's all my fault. I messed up everything. The days have blurred together I don't know how long I've been here. I was released from the hospital after a weak stay when they determined I was not suicidal just emotionally broken. After I laid in my bed I haven't gotten out since. I spend my days crying and staring at the wall I barely even eat. I'm just so tired. I curl up into my bed and let sleep take me. I arrive in my house in my office surrounded by paperwork. This has to be a dream. There is no way I can keep my job after I let the first daughter get murdered. I'll be lucky if I get a case as a mall cop. I hear voices so I decide to check it out. As I get closer to the voice, I recognize it as Dare. He is breaking even in my dreams. I search through the main level where I find him playing princess with a little girl. She is absolutely gorgeous. "Mommy I need you the king is trying to put me in the dungeon." Did she just call me mommy?"

"No one puts my princess in the dungeon."

"Princess Armani, do you want to tell our queen what you have done to earn time in a dungeon?"

"Nope." We both burst out laughing. I hear the door open and see several figures enter. My brain doesn't process who and I don't bother looking up. "Ava." I hear my mother calling my name. I want Dare. "Ava baby, you have to get up. There are a bunch of children out there that you need to find." I hear my father say. "Your brothers are worried about you." I have a brother. I don't know who those other three are. I hear more shuffling in the room and my mother excited says. "Hey baby, It is so good to see you. You are exactly who she wants to see. Ava, you have a special visitor." I don't respond. I don't want any more visitors. I want to sit here and waste away. Why can't they just leave me alone? "Av, baby can you hear me?" I'm dreaming. Dare is dead. I watched him die. "Ava baby. I need you to look at me." I still don't move. "I need you to snap out of it A. I fought these last two months to get back to you. Now I need you to fight whatever is locking you in your head. I need you. I want you to fight for me like I fought for you. I saw our future. We have six beautiful children. Five boys and a girl. We filled up that castle you built. That won't happen if you don't come back to me. I have no reason to stay here if you leave me."

"Armani." Everyone gasps. "Ava baby you're here." I feel arms wrapping around me. "Who's Armani baby?' Asks Darrius. "Our daughter her name is Armani I saw her too." She loves being a princess but spends a lot of time in the dungeon she is going to be a handful. "You scared the shit out of me." Darrius lays his head into my lap and cries. "it will take more than just a beating for me to ever leave you. I love you, Ava."

"I love you too." He pulls me out of the bed and drags me to the shower. "I don't want to hurt your feelings but baby you stink. I am burning this gown." When was the last time I bathed I honestly can't remember. I think to myself. "Two weeks ago." I look at him wondering I said that out loud. "I could tell by your face you were trying to count the days." He strips my clothing and I look at him in awe. All of the bruising is gone. You would never think he was just released from the hospital. He is in perfect condition. It isn't until he reaches to pick me up that I realize he was just released from the hospital. "Oh no you don't."

"What's wrong I always shower with you."

"Yes, but now you are hurt and don't need to be picking up on nothing. You have freshly healed ribs Dare." "Yep, I'm in trouble you called me Dare."

"I always call you Dare." I look at him with my face pinched trying to figure out what he is talking about. "No. You call me Darrius or Mr. Jones. You only call me Dare when you are mad. Like it is an insult or something."

"You tripping. Move so I can wash my ass." I enter the shower and welcome the stinging pain of the hot water. I don't know how long I spend in the shower. I rub my skin raw. I hate to think of how upset my mom is. To have her children fighting and her daughter trapped in her head for two months has to be terrifying. I need to talk to my brothers. I exit the shower and throw on a jogging suit. Meeting Darrius in the kitchen. "We need to talk."

"Whatever I did I'm sorry and she is just an employee I swear."

"Who the fuck is she?"

"Never mind you were saying." I shoot daggers at him with my eyes. I'll go back to that later. "We need to talk to my brothers. I don't like having my family split. Yes, they were wrong, but I can't continue hurting my mother with this."

"Ava, they almost killed me. You may be ready to forgive them, but I can't right now. I'm sorry."

"I understand baby." I kiss him softly on his head before grabbing my keys and heading across town. Once I enter my parents gates, I see that my brothers are already here. I sit in my car or a little bit to compose myself before getting out. Once I have my mind straight, I enter the house. Everyone is gathered around the kitchen island. They freeze awkwardly once they realize who is here. My mom speaks first. "Ava baby you're here."

"Yeah, Momma, I came to talk to your sons. I can't stand dividing our family." I turn to face my brothers. "I appreciate your concern, but it is no longer needed. Honestly, do you think Mom and Dad would have let me move across the county if I couldn't handle myself? I am nowhere near the naïve eighteen-year-old girl who let home six years go. I have had my heartbroken enough times to know how to fix it on my own. The man you should have been worried about is yourselves. Arix, you trusted him enough to bring him home and make him apart of your family he should have been your first choice in a man for your only sister. And you two." I turn to face my oldest brothers. "Yall are almost thirty, but yall out hear fighting over hearsay shit. That's some bitch made shit. My momma ain't raise no punks. Next time you have a problem with the people I associate with see me about it or we will have a repeat of the interrogation room. Take some notes from baby boy he knows how to mind his business."

"What happed in the interrogation room?" Asks my momma. Arix, Junior and Tony shake their heads so fast their cheeks vibrate. "I had to show them just how well I can handle myself."

"So, you're why Junior booked extra massages

with his therapist. They told us it was some thugs in the holding cell."

"She is a thug Momma. We fought back and still got our asses kicked.

18

Chapter Eighteen

Chapter Eighteen

Darrius

I 've been home for two weeks now. I ended my lease with Aix last week sometime. I just don't feel comfortable there anymore. I have been slowly moving my things into Ava's without her noticing. She has been so focused on finding Dianne's kidnapper/murderer that everything else is an afterthought. The only thing I need is to set up my office, which I can't do because the only space left is the room next to her office in the basement. I need to get her out of the house. I call Payge and we decide she needs a spa day. After lots of arguing we finally get her to agree. I have to work fast though because I only have two hours. I call Aiden and I am pissed to see he called the other Moore men to help. I ignore them and tell Aid what needs to be done we get to work and burn though all this mess. I'm grateful they came, but it doesn't change a thing. My phone rings and I see it is Leslie. 'Yo, What's up."

"Yeah, I just received a copy of Reese Alexander's new manuscript."

"Ok forward it to me."

"I know you were in the hospital for a bit, but you have seen him sense he finished haven't you."

"Mr. Alexader and Is relationship is a little complicated right now for now all professional correspondences will be handled through you. I end the call and meet the worried gaze of Arix. "You're lucky I don't let my personal life affect my business. We then get back to work. After everything is unloaded and relatively put away, they leave me to finish up on my own. I am scared shitless when I hear Ava's voice. "Took you long enough."

"What?"

"I thought your office would be the first thing

you would have set up when you moved in." "You knew." "I've known since the first night when you moved in your toiletries. I am an FBI agent who specializes in the finer details. Did you really think I wouldn't notice when all your stuff just randomly started popping up in my house? You have your entire wardrobe stashed in the guest closet. I made space for you in my closet by the way." I can't help but laugh. I thought I was being sneaky. She's a better detective than I thought. "Thanks for including my brothers. I know you could have done all of this by yourself."

"I was tired of them walking on eggshells around me. We aren't best friends yet, but I don't hate them anymore either. I can understand their intents although the application was a little unorthodox. At least you know your brothers love you. I know some people who their family could care less who they dated good or bad. "I guess you're right I still at them to attend anger management classes. They cannot happen again to anyone. I go to agree until I get a phone call. "You answer that I have a body to find." I answer the phone making a mental note to check in on her later. "Darrius Jones speaking."

"Hello Mr. Jones. I'm with Ace construction just calling to see if we are still on for demolition tomorrow." I completely forgot about the storefront. "Yes sir. I will fax you the permits right now." I dig through the massive pile of paperwork on my desk before finding what I need. I send it off waiting for confirmation. "I got them. What time should we get there?"

"Meet me there around eight a.m. we can do a walk through, and I can walk you through the plans one more time."

"Sounds good to me. I'll see you tomorrow." I walk to Ava's office planning to check on her, but her door is locked, and it is the one room with a keypad besides the gun/panic room. I decide to take a shower and head to sleep instead.

I jump into the shower and my thoughts wader to a memory of one of the many times I took Ava in this very shower. The most memorable being Christmas eve, before everything went to shit. We knew that Christmas was going to be too hectic for us to sped any alone time together, so we decide to attempt to satisfy our desire for each other enough to last through dinner.

As flashes of the night flicker through my head

my dick begs for attention. I gently tug on it for relief, but my efforts only make it worse. I am reminded of the snug, warm feeling of Ava's pussy spasming on my dick after her explosive orgasm. I use my hand to mimic the motion of her hips as I bring myself to completion. Once I can't take anymore, I release my load onto the floor and nearly faint from the intensity. I haven't come in over two months. I don't allow myself to dwell on it too long I wash myself good before drying off and putting on some boxers.

It's not long after my head hits the pillow that sleep consumes me. Morning comes much too soon. I stretch a little before attempting to get out of bed. it's not until I reach my stomach to remove Ava as I usually have to that I realize she is not there. "Where the hell is that woman at?" I ask no one at all.

I jump out of bed and look around or her terrified that my nightmare has come true. It's when I reach her office, I realize what has happened. She never came to bed last night. Her office door is slightly ajar meaning she did leave at some point last night. I push it open to see her completely knocked out across her desk. Without thought I pull her up and begin to bring her to our room. When I go to exit the room, a picture catches my eye Dianne Williams first daughter of the United States. What shocks me is the word deceased written beneath her picture. That explains why she has been so stressed out about this case.

I kiss her forehead and proceed to tucking her into bed. After she is comfortable, I get dressed and head out. I can feel that the day is going to be a long one as soon as I park my car. Apparently, word has gotten out about what I plan to open, and a small protest is being held in front of the store. Thankfully, there is a back entrance.

Once I am inside, I track down the supervisor so that we can begin working. Th day drags by with constant interruptions by the protestors. Some have seemed to forgotten that it's a construction site and just barged in with no safety gear. Enough for OSHA to shut us down. I call the police and have the protest broken up. The right to protest is all good until it gets someone hurt. Once I am happy with the progress, I call it a day.

I stop by subway for Ava and me some dinner, when I get the sense, someone is watching me. I look around but no one catches my eye, so I rush it off. Once I get on the highway headed back home, I see a black van following behind me. What is going on? I take a few random exits and turns losing the van before continuing to my destination. I reach the house all alone or so I thought. As I pass the gate, I realize we have a guest. The black van. I exit the car cautiously wishing at this moment my trigger-happy partner was at my side. The driver exits the car at the same time.

"About time. I've been out here forever. Can you tell Ava she can stop looking for me now."

Chapter Ninteen

Chapter Nineteen

Ava I wake to the shock of my life. "Am I dead?"

"NopeI sit up and gather my bearings. The child that I have cried over for the past two months is sitting across from me "You're not dead."

"No. and you can't take a hint. I thought you would leave me alone once you thought was dead, but that didn't happen it just made it worse. You just couldn't do like the others. You are the only person who was intent on finding me dead or alive."

"Because it was my job. You are the first daughter

what did you expect me to do. Your dad has called me almost every day during the investigation. "

"Yes, but once it was declared a homicide it was given to a new department, yet you still kept looking. Why?"

"After the initial shock wore off I began to think this was all too easy. So, I went back through the evidence and concluded that this was all very juvenile The text messages and the emails. The gift was the only thing that confused me. Why?"

"I needed you to be suspicious of my father. If you trusted him then he would find me."

"He did that on his own."

"Do you know how hard it is to hide from you for this long?" "I was almost captured by your team several times. You are a damn good agent. Good thing my dad underestimated you."

"What do you mean by that?"

"My father chooses the agents he thinks won't find anything. Because of your pas he thought you would be vulnerable and allow him to find me first. The only reason yall was called is because of Amanda. She actually loves me even though she isn't my real mother."

"Amanda isn't your mom?' "Nope my dad killed

her. Its why I ran. I needed justice for my mom. I couldn't get that living under the same roof as her killer." Dianne, I mean Diamonique sits me down and tells me exactly the type of man her father is. How is it that he was so charming he was able to be elected president twice. She tells me about the abuse her and Amanda have to endure every day. It makes me wonder what would possess Amanda to want to bring her back into that environment. The more I talk with her the more I like her. Her rough attitude is a shield from being hurt. Her dad has made her into a shell. I will get her justice. "I have a plan, but you won't like it. I will bring up charges on your dad. I need you to do something you probably really don't want to do." She looks at me with concern "And that would be?"

"You have to go home."

"I'm not going back there are you crazy. ' Just listen. To make sure your dad goes to jail for a long time we have to get a confession. He will do whatever he can to keep you quiet, so you have to be smart. You know him better than anyone else. How do we catch him?"

"Well, he loves to gloat about how he'll get away with it while he beats me. He even told me that I would end up just like my mother. Dead. It's how I found out Amanda wasn't my mother. I asked her about it, and she doesn't know where my mother is. I went looking through his things one day and I found the box of everything I gave you.' "Good so hear is the plan." I then explain to her exactly how we will take her father down. I then all up my team and let them know. We put everything in motion and pray for the desired outcome. Three weeks later. I exit the cab and nod to the agent at the gate. I calmly make my way inside and join in the line or the tour. As we wait Diamonique passes with her father. I adjust the wig and glasses ensuring don't recognize me. she spots me in the crowd and gives me the signal. I calmly steady myself and follow the crowd. I assume everything is going to plan until I hear gunshots. Everyone is confused ad begins to run out. I duck into a bathroom and quickly pit on my vest before making my way through the building finding the shooter. I realize what happened when I reach the oval office. When I enter the room, the president is laying in a pool of his own blood and the first lady is aiming a gun at Diamonique. "Put the gun down."

"Of course, you're hear."

"Amanda. Just put the gun down and let's talk."

"No. I'm done talking. I have played the dutiful wife for him too long. He just had to get greedy. We would have been lounging on an unknown island with billions of dollars in the bank and this little bitch in foster care had he stuck to the plan. No, he just had to be president. She turns to look at me. "Do really look like someone's first lady?" The pristine face I knew is now replaced with a long scar down the left side of her face. Her full checks are now sunk in, and her eyes are cold and dead. "What did he do to you?"

"You really are a dumb bitch."

"He didn't do anything that I didn't tell him to. I'm not a lapdog I'm the HBIC always have been you were just too blind to see it."

"Malcom's ass would still be just a thug if it weren't for me. I made him. Everything was fine until this little bitch came back. She was supposed to be dead. She just happened to be gone when I got to her room. So, I paid to have her found and killed. I was waiting for the call that they found her in a known drug area dead from overdose. What I got instead was that she vanished. I had to play the role. While my men looked for you.

Imagine my shock when she just walks through the front door like nothing happened."

"Now, here is how it's going to go. You will leave her and let me finish what I started, or you will end up just like him."

"Here is a better idea you drop the gun and spend the rest of your life rotting in prison."

"Yeah, not gonna happen" She then aims and fires.

To Be Continued